KRISTY AND THE CAT BURGLAR

Ann M. Martin

AN
APPLE
PAPERBACK

SCHOLASTIC INC.
New York Toronto London Auckland Sydney

Cover art Ed Acuña

ISBN 0-590-05976-9

12 11 10 9 8 7 6 5 4 3 2 1   8 9/9 0 1 2 3/0

Printed in the U.S.A.   40

First Scholastic printing, August 1998

*The author gratefully acknowledges
Ellen Miles
for her help in
preparing this manuscript.*

KRISTY AND THE
CAT BURGLAR

CHAPTER 1

"My — mother — said — to — pick — the — very — next — ONE!" Karen tapped David Michael's fist with her own. "You're 'it.' Remember, you have to count to a hundred and fifty by fives before you can start looking for us."

"I know, I know," said David Michael, my younger brother. He and Karen Brewer, our stepsister, are the same age (seven), but Karen can be bossy.

The three of us (I'm Kristy Thomas) were in our backyard. It was one of those warm, lazy late-summer afternoons, and the sun was just starting to sink. It had been a beautiful day, and we'd spent most of it outdoors. When Karen had suggested a game of hide-and-seek, David Michael and I agreed right away. None of us was in any hurry to go inside. We had plenty of time before supper.

"Okay, here I go!" David Michael cried. He

leaned against a tree, hiding his face in his arms. Then he began to count, "Five, ten, fifteen —"

Karen and I grinned at each other, then took off in opposite directions. I glanced back once, in time to see her diving behind a giant fern. *Good spot*, I thought. *Now, where am I going to hide?* I ran toward a huge, old tree trunk. *That'll do*, I said to myself. By then, David Michael was up to ninety-five. Not a moment to waste. I ducked behind the tree and crouched down.

I listened to David Michael counting and thought about all the games of hide-and-seek I've played over the years. Long ago, it was just me and my older brothers, Charlie and Sam. They were the ones who taught me all the important kid games. Then David Michael was born, and not long after that everything changed. My dad walked out on our family, and the fun times were over for awhile.

But my mom, otherwise known as Superwoman (secret identity: Elizabeth Thomas), held our family together. She was amazing. She made sure we always had food to eat and clothes to wear. She also taught us to enjoy life and to go for whatever we want out of it.

Mom deserves the best, and she found it when she met Watson Brewer, who is now my stepdad. He's an awesome guy, though I'll admit that I didn't recognize that right away.

Sweet, funny, caring — you couldn't ask for a nicer man. And on top of it all, he's an actual millionaire.

Karen is Watson's daughter from his first marriage. I adore having a little sister, so I'm lucky to have two! Besides Karen, there's Emily Michelle, who's just a toddler. She was born in Vietnam. Mom and Watson adopted her not long after they were married. (Soon after Emily arrived, my grandmother Nannie moved in with us, to help out.)

Watson also has a son, a four-year-old named Andrew. He's a great kid, and I miss him a lot. Right now he's living with his mom and stepdad in Chicago. They're spending six months there. He and Karen used to split their time between their mom and Watson. Now (temporarily) Andrew's mostly with his mom, and Karen's mostly with us.

We all live in Watson's gigantic mansion, which is way across town from where I grew up. ("Town" is Stoneybrook, Connecticut, where I've lived all my life.) I'm thirteen now and in the eighth grade at Stoneybrook Middle School. Most of my friends still live in my old neighborhood, but I see them pretty often, since I'm over there three times a week for BSC meetings. The BSC is the Baby-sitters Club, and I never miss a meeting because I happen to be president. But more about that later.

David Michael finished counting. Then he hollered, "Ready or not, here I come!" and started to run around the yard, looking for me and Karen. I hunkered down, hiding as well as I could. If he didn't find me after a reasonable amount of time, I'd give him a little clue by coughing or rustling leaves. Sometimes kids can become frustrated if the game is too hard. I wanted the day to end on a fun note, not with tears.

"Boo!"

I almost jumped out of my skin. I'd been keeping an eye on David Michael's progress, so I hadn't even noticed someone else creeping up behind me.

"Cary!" I said. "What are you doing here?" It was Cary Retlin, who's in my class at school. He's a practical joker extraordinaire, and I've learned to watch out for his tricks. Cary's always up to something, and it pays to be on the alert when you're around him. The BSC has had more than one run-in with Cary. One time he even challenged us to a mystery war. I can't say who won, since it never exactly ended.

"I could ask you the same thing," Cary said, lifting an eyebrow.

Suddenly I felt foolish. There I was, squatting in the dirt, while Cary stood, looking down at me. Normally I'm a confident person. I'm sure of myself and don't hesitate to offer

4

my opinions. Like Karen, I am even bossy at times. But something about Cary Retlin makes me feel awkward. I stood up. "I guess that was a silly question," I said. Our yard backs up to a wooded area that runs past Cary's house too.

"I guess so," he agreed.

By then, Karen and David Michael had abandoned the game and joined us.

"What are those for?" asked Karen, pointing to the binoculars that hung from a strap around Cary's neck.

Aren't kids great? If they're curious about something, they just ask. I'd been wondering about the binoculars myself.

"I'm bird-watching," said Cary, lifting that eyebrow again. He shrugged off the backpack he carried and, unzipping it, pulled out a book. "Today I saw one of these," he said, riffling through the pages to find a picture of a nondescript brown bird, "and a couple of these." He pointed to another picture that looked almost the same to me.

"Cool," said David Michael.

"I didn't know you were so interested in nature," I said to Cary.

"Oh, I'm a regular Audubon," he replied with a smirk.

Hmm. Cary is full of surprises. Just then, Karen tugged on my hand. I looked down at her. "Is it your turn to be 'it'?" I asked.

"I don't want to play anymore," she said. "Let's explore the woods."

"Okay," I agreed. "See you, Cary."

"Not if I see you first," he said, making a little pistol out of his hand and pointing it at me.

What a wise guy. He always has to have the last word.

With Karen leading the way (she's fearless and loves the woods), the three of us pushed on. "Let's go check out the spooky house," she said.

"The what?" I asked.

"You know, that big old house in the middle of the woods. It looks like nobody lives there, but Hannie's dad says somebody does." (Hannie is Hannie Papadakis, a seven-year-old neighbor who is one of Karen's best friends.)

I knew what Karen was talking about. "Oh, the place with the stone walls?" I asked.

"And the cool windows," added David Michael.

We emerged from the woods onto a narrow road. This was the private road the "spooky house" is on. There are only a few houses along it. Since there was very little traffic, it was safe to walk right down the middle of the road, as if it were our own private path.

"Car!" Karen sang out. We all moved over to the left-hand side of the road. A white car cruised slowly past, and I saw that it was from the Stoneybrook Police Department. I realized that the driver was someone I know: Sergeant Johnson. He's a detective and a good friend to the BSC. I waved, but I guess he didn't see me, because he didn't wave back.

"There's the wall!" shouted Karen as she ran toward a driveway off to the right.

Sure enough, a stone wall, taller than I am, ran along the side of the road, outlining the entrance to the driveway. Near the entrance was a black mailbox. I didn't even have time to stop and check for a name, because Karen was pulling me along.

"Let's go see the mansion," said Karen. "Can we?" She tugged on my arm.

"I don't know," I said. "I have a feeling this wall means we're not supposed to go in there."

"But there's no gate across the driveway," David Michael pointed out. He and Karen were already in motion, making their way toward the mansion.

"It's somebody's private property all the same," I protested. But my heart wasn't in it. I was just as curious as David Michael and Karen. And I couldn't help following them down the driveway — *just for a little peek,* I told myself. I'd seen the mansion before, but I hadn't been there for a long time.

We walked down the driveway, which wound through the woods. Suddenly, it opened out into a large clearing. In the middle of the clearing stood an impressive stone house. It looked almost like an old castle, with ivy crawling all over it and dozens of leaded-glass windows. Nobody was stirring, and I didn't see any cars or other signs of life. There was something almost creepy about the place, especially at this hour of the day.

"Okay, we've seen it," I said. "Now it's time to go home."

"But —" Karen began.

Just then, a shot rang out.

Really! I know it sounds dramatic, but that's exactly what happened. And even though I haven't heard too many actual gunshots, somehow I was pretty sure that's what I had just heard.

"Let's go!" I said. "Now!" I grabbed Karen with one hand and David Michael with the other, and we started to run toward the road. Fast.

A loud siren began to wail. I ran even faster. Something was happening at that house, and I didn't want to be any part of it. Was the alarm going off because we'd walked too near the house? Or was it something more serious?

Then I heard another high wail — the sound of police sirens. They were coming closer by the second. And then they stopped. I heard slamming doors and voices. I tightened my hold on Karen and David Michael and pulled them down the driveway. All I wanted was to get out of there.

We were nearing the stone wall, the road beyond it, and safety. We passed the mailbox, and I had just begun to loosen my grip, when suddenly a male voice rang out behind us.

"DON'T MOVE!"

CHAPTER 2

I froze, and made sure David Michael and Karen froze too. My heart was thudding in my chest. Who was behind us? Was he holding a gun? More than anything, I wanted to be somewhere else. Where? I didn't care. Algebra class. The North Pole. Anywhere except in the driveway of a spooky house where a gun had just been shot off.

"Kristy?"

I turned and heaved a huge sigh of relief. A tall, black-haired man was standing behind me. It was Sergeant Johnson.

"Oh, man, am I glad to see you." I breathed a sigh of relief.

"I can't say the feeling is mutual," he said sternly. "I like you, Kristy, but I'm sorry to see you here. A baby-sitter and two kids do not belong at a crime scene."

"Crime scene?" repeated David Michael. "Cool!"

Sergeant Johnson shook his head. "Not cool," he said. "That alarm you heard could mean that there's a burglar nearby — and he could be armed."

"So what if he has arms?" asked Karen. "Everybody has arms." She waved hers around for emphasis.

"He means the guy might have a gun," hissed David Michael. "Don't you know anything?"

I thought of mentioning the shot I had heard, but Sergeant Johnson was in a hurry.

"Follow me," he ordered. He led the way to his squad car, which was parked just out of sight in a little turnaround area down the driveway. He opened the back door and ushered us inside. "I want you all to sit tight until I come for you," he said, closing the car door behind us. Just then, another squad car pulled up and a policewoman climbed out. I didn't recognize her and figured she must be new to the force. She had dark hair and a small, pale, round face, and she looked very serious as she asked Sergeant Johnson a few questions about what was going on.

After they'd spoken for a moment, Sergeant Johnson leaned down to talk to me through the open window. He gave me a quick introduction to the policewoman, whose name was Officer Hopkins, and sure enough, she was new

11

to Stoneybrook. "We're going to check out the house," he said. "Stay right here."

I nodded. No way was I moving, not if some criminal was running around with a gun. I had two young kids with me, kids I was responsible for. I was more than happy to obey Sergeant Johnson's orders.

Within a few minutes, Sergeant Johnson and the other officer were back. Sergeant Johnson climbed into the front seat and started talking into the radio. Most of what he said was in numbers. You know what I mean. Like on the cop shows, when the police officer says, "We have a twelve forty-eight here with multiple sixties and a four twenty-nine."

After he finished, Sergeant Johnson turned to look at us. "I just called for more officers," he explained. "There's definitely been some sort of break-in. Nobody's home, but the back door is open. We'll have to check it out more thoroughly."

Just then, another car pulled up. It wasn't a police car though. Just a little red sedan. A man in a dark blue uniform jumped out. "What's going on?" he asked. "My name's Jack Fenton. I'm the security guard for this place." He showed Officer Hopkins some ID. "Has there been a break-in?"

"It seems as if there has," said Officer Hopkins. "Were you on duty today?"

He nodded, looking terrified. "Yes," he said. "I usually check the place out three times a day. But just as I was starting my rounds here today I had an emergency call about my wife being taken to the hospital. So I took off. Oh, man, I don't believe this!"

"That's interesting," said Sergeant Johnson, who had climbed out of his car by then. "I had a call right around that time too. An anonymous call, telling me to check out this house."

Have I mentioned that Sergeant Johnson has the clearest, bluest eyes I've ever seen? Well, he does. But at that moment, they looked clouded, almost gray. There was something about that phone call that bothered him.

The security guard groaned. "I'm going to be out of a job," he said. "What was stolen? Have you checked the vault yet?"

"Vault?" asked Officer Hopkins. She exchanged a look with Sergeant Johnson. "Maybe you'd better show us where that is. We were just about to do a more complete check of the place. Our backup should be here any minute."

After making one more number-filled radio call, Sergeant Johnson and the other two took off toward the house, but not before he warned me again to stay in the car.

They returned a few minutes later, just as another squad car was pulling up. A short, balding officer jumped out of the car and approached the group. I didn't recognize him either. Another new addition to the Stoneybrook police? He nodded at Sergeant Johnson and Officer Hopkins. "I'm Sergeant Winters," he said to Jack Fenton. "What's going on here? And who are these kids?" He frowned at me.

Officer Hopkins jumped in to update Sergeant Winters. She introduced Jack Fenton, and explained why "those kids" were in Sergeant Johnson's car. She explained about the two phone calls and the break-in. Then she told him that Jack Fenton had wanted to check out a vault he knew about.

"And?" asked Sergeant Winters.

"The diamonds are missing," reported Jack Fenton. He looked miserable. "Mr. Golem — that's Reinhart Golem, the owner of this place — has been keeping a bag of extremely valuable diamonds in a vault. He felt they were much safer here than they would be in a bank, since this house is so out-of-the-way."

I gasped, and so did Karen and David Michael. Diamonds? This was getting more interesting by the minute.

"We told him to put them in a bank." Jack Fenton was still talking. "My boss told him it was a mistake to have them here. But would he listen? No, he said he knew best. But who's going to be in trouble now? Not Reinhart Golem, that's for sure. No, it's going to be *my* —"

Sergeant Winters interrupted him. "Has the crime scene been secured?" he asked sharply, turning to the other police officers. "Have you dusted for fingerprints?"

Sergeant Johnson and Officer Hopkins admitted that they hadn't.

"Let's do this right, shall we?" asked Sergeant Winters. "A crime of this magnitude needs to be handled with organization and correct police procedure. Sergeant Johnson, have you begun to fill out a report?"

Sergeant Johnson shook his head. "Not yet. I was just about to." He opened the car door and reached in for a clipboard that was sitting on the front passenger seat. "Grandstanding as usual," he muttered.

I knew he was talking about Sergeant Winters, but I wasn't sure what he meant. Was it "grandstanding" to act as if you were the only person who knew how to do things right and to walk into the middle of an event and start criticizing everyone? If so, I had to agree with Sergeant Johnson. Sergeant Winters was definitely grandstanding.

Sergeant Johnson perched on the seat of his car and began to fill out a form.

"Has the owner of the house been contacted?" Sergeant Winters asked.

"Not yet," answered Officer Hopkins. "I suggested that we do that, but Sergeant Johnson said to wait."

"Only until we returned to the car," said Sergeant Johnson, clearly exasperated. "I said I'd call when we were back at my radio." He frowned at Officer Hopkins, and I did too. Why was she trying to make him look bad in front of Officer Winters?

Jack Fenton stepped forward. "I have a number for Reinhart Golem," he said. He held out a slip of paper he'd taken from his wallet. "I've never even met the guy. He spends most of his time over in Europe or somewhere. But this is supposedly the number where he can be reached in an emergency." He handed the paper to Sergeant Johnson.

Sergeant Johnson took it and reached for his cell phone. He punched in the number and waited. After a pause, he left a brief message with his name and phone number. "No answer," he explained after he'd hung up. "Just a voice-mail message. I'll try again later." He stuck the paper in his pocket.

"What else do you know about this Reinhart Golem?" Sergeant Winters asked Jack Fenton.

Fenton shrugged. "Not much," he admitted. "He's rich, that's for sure," he said, waving a hand around at the mansion, the private driveway, the stone walls. "But nobody seems to know how he made his fortune."

Sergeant Johnson cleared his throat as if he were going to speak. But then he shook his head and began filling in the form on his clipboard. I had the feeling somehow that he knew more about Golem than Fenton did.

"He's a loner," Fenton continued. "Never married, from what I hear. And, like I said, he doesn't spend much time around here. It's a waste, if you ask me. You should see all the nice stuff in that house. A full-size whirlpool bath, large-screen TV, the works!"

"Why does he have a picture of a red cat on his mailbox?" I asked. I don't know what came over me. The question just flew out before I could stop myself.

"A cat?" asked Sergeant Johnson, wheeling around to look at me. "When did you see that?"

"Today," I answered, "just before you told us to freeze. I forgot all about it until now."

"Well, I'm glad you mentioned it," said Sergeant Johnson. "That is very, very interesting news. That cat was not there before. This means the Cat Burglar may be involved."

"A cat burglar?" asked Officer Hopkins.

"No, *the* Cat Burglar," Sergeant Johnson corrected her. "This wouldn't be the first heist he's pulled around here. We haven't been able to find out much about him. All we know is that the Cat Burglar robs the homes of the very rich and leaves a stenciled silhouette of a red cat behind as a calling card." He rubbed his hands together. "If we could catch him, we would make a lot of people happy. Including some of the biggest police forces on the East Coast."

"Are you sure this cat picture appeared today?" asked Sergeant Winters.

Sergeant Johnson nodded, and Jack Fenton jumped in to back him up. "I know *I* never saw it before," he said.

Wow. This was exciting. Just then, I saw a movement out of the corner of my eye and turned to look. I caught — just barely — Cary Retlin ducking behind a toolshed. He seemed interested in what was going on, but not interested enough to show himself to the police.

I wondered about him. Could he have had anything to do with this? I could imagine Cary setting off a burglar alarm just for kicks. But shooting a gun? Stealing diamonds? Those activities were a little out of Cary's line. Still, seeing him lurking made me curious about what he was *really* doing with those binoculars. Was it only birds he was interested in?

"Kristy!" David Michael was tugging on my sleeve. "Can we go? It's going to be dark soon."

18

"I want to go home," Karen chimed in. "Do we have to stay?"

I looked at Sergeant Johnson, who was still filling out the incident form. "Do you think it's safe to go?" I asked him.

He nodded. "I'm sure that burglar is miles away by now," he said, rubbing his eyes. "But I'll tell you what. How would you like a ride home in a real patrol car? Just to be on the safe side." He winked at me.

"Yea!" cried David Michael.

"Can you make the siren go off?" asked Karen.

"Too noisy," said Sergeant Johnson apologetically. "But how about if I make the lights flash?"

"Cool," said David Michael and Karen together.

I gave Sergeant Johnson a thankful glance. I'd been a little nervous about walking back home through the woods, now that dusk was falling.

Sergeant Johnson stepped out of the car. "I'm going to run these kids home," he told the other officers. "I'll finish up this form when I come back. And if there's any fingerprinting to do —"

"We'll take care of it," said Sergeant Winters, interrupting. He and Officer Hopkins exchanged a look.

"Oh. All right." said Sergeant Johnson, sounding surprised. "I'll be back in a few minutes."

"No need to rush," said Sergeant Winters coolly.

What was going on here? There was definitely tension between Sergeant Johnson and the other two officers. I felt bad for Sergeant Johnson, but he seemed to shrug everything off. He climbed back into the car, started it up, and drove down the drive. He lingered near the gate, checking out the red cat on the mailbox, but all he said was, "Hmm, interesting."

"What about the lights?" David Michael reminded him, as Sergeant Johnson turned onto the road.

"Coming right up." Sergeant Johnson reached out to push a button. It was dark enough by then so that the lights lit up the woods around us.

"Yes!" cried David Michael.

"This is so neat," said Karen. "I can't wait to tell my friends all about it."

I couldn't wait either. My fellow BSC members would be very, very interested in the day's events. We love mysteries, and there was no question that a burglary involving valuable diamonds, a missing security guard, a gunshot, and a criminal who called himself the Cat Burglar would qualify.

CHAPTER 3

"Wait, back up. *What* did you say that guy's name was?"

"Reinhart Golem," I repeated. I spread out my hands. "I know, I know, it's a weird name. But *everything* that happened yesterday was pretty weird."

It was Wednesday, and my friends and I were in the midst of a BSC meeting. I was filling everyone in on the events of the evening before.

Maybe I should pause here and explain a little about the BSC. We are a group of friends, all very different but with one thing in common: we love kids and we love to baby-sit. We are caring, responsible, enthusiastic sitters — the kind kids *and* parents love. When we first started the club, we advertised with fliers and signs, but now we hardly ever have to. Word of mouth is our best advertising.

It all began one afternoon when my mom

was trying to find a sitter for David Michael. She made phone call after phone call, with no luck. That's when I had this majorly incredible brainstorm (the first of many, if I do say so myself). What if parents could call one number and be sure of finding a good sitter?

The rest, as they say, is history. I asked a few friends to form a sitting business with me, and over time we've grown. We now have seven regular members plus two associate members and one honorary member. We meet (at least, the regular members do) every Monday, Wednesday, and Friday afternoon from five-thirty until six. Parents can call us during those times to set up jobs.

We keep a record book, with schedules and client information; a club notebook, in which we write up our jobs so that every sitter is up-to-date on every client; and a treasury, into which we pay dues every Monday to cover club costs. And we each have a Kid-Kit to bring on jobs — a box filled with puzzles, toys, games, and markers. Kid-Kits are a big hit with our charges.

One last brag: All of the above were ideas of mine. More brainstorms. I can't help it. If I were a cartoon, I'd always be pictured with a lightbulb over my head. My friends tease me about it. But they know the BSC is the best club ever.

We happen to be pretty good detectives too. We've helped to solve quite a few mysteries. (That's how we became such good friends with Sergeant Johnson.) One of my favorite memories involves the time I helped find a missing child. We work together on every case, but certain cases will always make me think of the BSC members most responsible for solving them.

For example, the art-related mystery Claudia solved. That's Claudia Kishi, the vice-president of the BSC. (She was elected to that post unanimously, mainly because she has her own phone and a private phone line, essential to our business.) Claudia is Japanese-American, with long black hair and almond-shaped eyes. She *loves* art. She's happiest when she has a paintbrush or a sculpting tool in her hand. So it makes sense that she was the one to figure out who had stolen some valuable coins from the Stoneybrook Art Museum. Now she's an honorary trustee at the museum.

Claudia still lives in the house in which she grew up — the one across the street from my old house. (I've known Claudia since we were in diapers.) Her mom is the head librarian at the Stoneybrook Public Library; her dad is a partner in an investment firm; and her older sister, Janine, is a genius. Really! Janine's in high school, but she's already taking college courses.

23

Claudia, on the other hand, does not do all that well in school. In fact, she even had to go back to seventh grade for awhile, but I'm thrilled to report that she has now returned to eighth. She's not dumb; she just doesn't care much about facts and figures.

Besides art, Claudia's other true loves are 1) junk food (show her a Ring-Ding and watch her eyes light up) and 2) Nancy Drew mysteries (maybe that's why she's such a good detective). Both of the above are frowned upon by her parents. One is junk food for the body, according to them, and the other is junk food for the brain. But that doesn't stop Claudia. She always has several books hidden away in her room, and she supplies the most awesome munchies for club meetings. That day she'd brought out a bag of caramel-nut popcorn, plus a package of chocolate wafer cookies.

Oh, and a bag of salsa-flavored corn chips for Stacey. Stacey McGill, the BSC's treasurer, is Claudia's best friend. She's blonde and blue-eyed and sophisticated. Fashion is not my strong point — far from it. In fact, I hardly ever wear anything other than jeans and a T-shirt. So I couldn't tell you exactly what Stacey's style *is*, but I do know she has it. Tons of it. I think it might be partly because she grew up in Manhattan. Her dad still lives there (her parents are divorced) so Stacey continues to make regular pilgrimages to all her favorite stores. Consequently, she dresses way better than any eighth-grader I've ever seen.

Stacey's best mystery ever? It must be the time she helped to catch a counterfeiter. Pretty cool, huh? It all started when she used a counterfeit bill (she thought it was real) to buy some earrings. And by the time it was over, a big-time criminal had been put away for a long, long time. Go, Stacey!

Oh, about those chips: Claudia always makes sure to have sugar-free snacks on hand for Stacey. Why? Because Stacey has diabetes, a disease that prevents her body from processing sugars correctly. If she isn't careful about what she eats and when she eats, she could get very, very sick. Plus, she has to test her blood sugar and give herself injections of insulin (a substance her body should make but doesn't) every single day. I think I'd be whining all the time if I had to do that, but Stacey rarely complains.

Just as she was helping herself to some chips, the phone rang. Stacey picked it up. "Hello, Baby-sitters Club," she said. She listened for a moment. "Sure, Dr. Johanssen," she continued. "We'll see who's free and call you right back, okay?" She hung up and turned to

Mary Anne Spier, who was sitting next to her on Claudia's bed. "Thursday afternoon?" she asked, raising her eyebrows.

Mary Anne scanned a page in the club record book. "You, Abby, or Mal," she said.

"Eye doctor," Mal piped up.

"Special soccer practice," said Abby.

"Me, then," said Stacey, reaching for the phone to call Dr. Johanssen back. I knew she was happy to have the job. Charlotte Johanssen is her favorite charge.

As you can probably tell, we have our BSC system down to a routine. Mary Anne didn't need to explain that "You, Abby, or Mal" meant that her schedule showed those members as the only free sitters for Thursday. And Mal and Abby didn't have to go into detail about why they couldn't take the job. It's all understood.

Also, nobody has to worry about Mary Anne making a scheduling mistake. As the BSC's secretary, she never has. She is neat and precise and very good at her job. That's not to say that Mary Anne is a robot. Far from it. She's the most sensitive person I know, and she has a very romantic nature (just ask her boyfriend, Logan Bruno!). Mary Anne's favorite mystery would probably be one she helped solve not long ago, involving a special music box and a secret romance. ("Sigh!" as Mary Anne would say.)

Mary Anne looks a little like me: We're both short for our age and have brown hair and brown eyes. But, while we've been best friends forever (she's another friend who goes way back to diaper times), our personalities couldn't be more different. Mary Anne is shy, quiet, and very sweet. I guess we complement each other. I am extremely lucky to have her for a best friend.

Mary Anne has another best friend, who happens to A) live in California and B) be her sister. See, Mary Anne was brought up as an only child, with just her father for a parent, because Mary Anne's mom died when Mary Anne was a baby. Mr. Spier did a good job of bringing up a daughter on his own (although he was a little too strict at times, in my opinion), but it can't have been easy. That's why it was so wonderful when he hooked up with an old flame from high school, a woman who had moved to California, married, and started a family, then divorced and returned to Stoneybrook with her two kids, Dawn and Jeff. Dawn and Mary Anne became best friends even before their parents married — and now they're sisters too. But Dawn, like her younger brother, Jeff, never truly came to love living in Connecticut, so they now spend most of their time with their dad in California. Dawn just spent the summer in Stoneybrook, though, which was great, since I know Mary Anne misses her.

Dawn was a member of the BSC when she lived here full-time. As the alternate officer she was always ready to step in if one of the officers had to miss a meeting. She's our honorary member now. Her old job is filled by Abby Stevenson, the BSC's newest member.

Abby and her twin sister, Anna, recently moved to Stoneybrook from Long Island. Their mom is a high-powered editor at a big publishing house in New York. Their dad? Well, he died in a car crash a few years ago. This has been really hard for Abby, and she misses him all the time. But she's full of jokes and fun, and she's always clowning around. Except, that is, when she's on the playing field or the track. Abby's a star athlete. A love for sports is something she and I have in common. In fact, Abby helps me coach Kristy's Krushers, a softball team I put together for little kids.

Even though Abby hasn't lived here long, she's definitely done her share of BSC detective work. Recently, she helped to solve one of our most exciting mysteries ever when she figured out the truth about a secret society at a local country club.

Abby and her sister are identical twins. Both have dark, curly hair and bad eyesight (they always wear either glasses or contacts). But we have no trouble telling them apart. Anna is much quieter and more serious, especially when it comes to her passion: music. She's an awesome violin player. In fact, she's so devoted to practicing that she turned us down when we invited her to join the BSC.

Abby and the rest of us are thirteen and in the eighth grade. But we have two members who are younger, our junior officers, Mallory Pike and Jessica Ramsey. They're best friends and both are eleven and in the sixth grade.

They may be young, but they're excellent detectives. Jessi discovered the true identity of a "dance-school phantom," and Mallory once helped solve a mystery involving a ghost cat (spooky!). They're also excellent sitters, even though their parents won't let them sit at night (except for their own siblings) until they're older.

Mal, who has reddish-brown hair, freckles, and braces (and hates all three), comes from a huge family. She has seven younger brothers and sisters! Jessi, who has cocoa-brown skin and the lean, strong body of a dancer (she studies ballet seriously), has a baby brother and a younger sister.

That's it, except for our associate members, who help out when we have more jobs than we can handle. (They've also helped out with a mystery or two.) One of them is Shannon Kilbourne, who lives in my neighborhood. The other is Logan Bruno, Mary Anne's boyfriend.

It was fun to look around the room and think about past mysteries we've solved, but day-dreaming wasn't getting me anywhere when it came to our latest mystery. Who had shot off that gun? Where were the diamonds? And why were Sergeant Winters and Officer Hopkins treating Sergeant Johnson so oddly? I was dying to find out the answers — and maybe I'd have the chance to start the next day, when I would go to the police station. That reminded me that I hadn't told my friends yet about the latest development.

"Sergeant Johnson called me this morning and asked if I could go down to the station to-morrow. I guess he wants to question me or something," I said just as our meeting was ending. "And I bet Cary Retlin will be there too. Sergeant Johnson asked me if I'd seen anyone else around that evening, and I told him about our bird-watching friend."

Mary Anne, supportive as always, offered to meet me after my appointment with Sergeant Johnson. Claudia said she'd come too. I accepted. After all, solving a mystery this big would take all the help I could find. Thank goodness I didn't have to look far for good help.

CHAPTER 4

Thursday

I smell trouble! I tried to warn Charlotte, but she's so excited about her new "career." And she knows about all the disastrous things that could happen. After all, she's read the book and seen the movie. But she's convinced it won't happen to her. So, here's to Charlotte the Spy. Let's keep our fingers crossed.

"Stacey McGill, my baby-sitter, looks awesome today, as always. Nobody else around here dresses as well as Stacey. Today she has on khaki pants and a white button-down blouse. She has a dark blue ribbon in her hair, and it kind of matches her eyes. Her shoes are brown lace-up boots, and —"

"Charlotte, what are you doing?" Stacey, who had heard Charlotte talking as she entered the Johanssens' kitchen, was now standing right in front of her, hands on hips. "And who are you talking to?" Stacey had arrived a little early (a BSC tradition) for her sitting job, and had just finished saying good-bye to Charlotte's mom, who was on her way to the hospital. (She's a doctor.)

"Oops," said Charlotte. "I guess I got a little carried away." She put down the small black case she'd been holding near her face. "I was — I was just thinking out loud."

"Oh, really?" asked Stacey, arching an eyebrow. She adores Charlotte. In fact, since they're both only children, they've kind of adopted each other. They call themselves "almost sisters." But something funny was going on, and Stacey could tell Charlotte wasn't being entirely honest with her. "I like your jeans, with the red sneakers and the red sweatshirt," Stacey said. "That's kind of a new look for you." She bent closer to look at something hanging from Charlotte's belt. "And what's that? A flashlight? Hmm. Interesting fashion statement."

"It's not a fashion statement," Charlotte replied. "It's a tool. I use it on my rounds —" She slapped a hand over her mouth.

"Rounds?" asked Stacey. She was beginning to understand. "What kind of rounds?" she asked innocently.

"Never mind," said Charlotte. "You wouldn't understand."

"Oh, no? Well, for your information, I've read *Harriet the Spy* more than once myself."

Charlotte gasped. "How did you know?"

"Just a lucky guess," said Stacey. She smiled to herself, remembering a short phase she'd gone through at about Charlotte's age. She'd had her own flashlight and her own red sweatshirt. "I just have one question," she said. "Where's your notebook?"

"I use this instead," said Charlotte proudly, holding up the black case. "It's a voice-activated tape recorder. Perfect for spyi — I mean, for dictating notes and stuff. My mom just bought a new one for work, and she passed this one on to me."

"Cool," said Stacey. "So, tell me about your rounds."

"You mean, you're not mad?"

"I'm not mad," said Stacey. "As long as you stay out of trouble. You do remember what happened to Harriet, don't you?"

Just in case you have no idea what this is all about, I'll explain. See, there's this book, *Harriet the Spy*. Louise Fitzhugh wrote it. It's about a girl who likes to spy on her friends and neighbors. She writes down all kinds of stuff about them in a notebook, because she wants to be a writer someday. Anyway, her friends end up reading the notebook. They're so hurt by what she has written about them that Harriet almost ends up losing her friends. Eventually, everything works out, but things look pretty bad for awhile. It's a great book, and if you haven't read it, you definitely should. Okay? Okay. Now, back to Stacey and Charlotte.

Charlotte grimaced. "That will never happen to me. I'm being really careful. Plus, I'm not writing anything down," she said, holding up the tape recorder. "So there's nothing for anyone to read."

"That doesn't mean people won't be angry if they find out you've been spying on them," Stacey pointed out.

"I'm not really spying. I'm just — watching."

Stacey smiled. "So, how long has this been going on?"

"It all started back when the recreation department sponsored that go-cart race. Remember? And I was building a go-cart with Vanessa and Becca?"

Vanessa is Mal's sister, and Becca is Jessi's. They're good friends of Charlotte.

"I remember," said Stacey.

"Well, Jackie and his brothers were building a go-cart too," Charlotte continued. She was talking about the Rodowsky boys, who live near Charlotte.

"I think I heard something about this," Stacey said, remembering some notes Mary Anne had written up in the club notebook.

"So you know that they spied on us," said Charlotte. "We were mad at first, and then we decided to spy on them. It was fun, and our go-carts came out great. They stole some ideas from us, and we stole from them."

Stacey knew she ought to point out that a little cooperation between teams might have had the same result, but Charlotte was too excited to listen. She was still telling her story. "Anyway, right about then I read *Harriet the Spy*. And then I rented the movie, and, well — " She shrugged and grinned. "I guess I have spy fever."

"I can see why," said Stacey.

"It's the coolest," said Charlotte. "I know about everything that's going on."

"Do your parents know what you're up to?"

"Sort of," said Charlotte, looking a little uncomfortable. "But a spy can't tell *all* her secrets, right?"

"That's true, I guess." It sounded to Stacey as if what Charlotte was doing was pretty innocent. But Stacey thought maybe she ought to be sure about that. "But you can share *some* of your secrets with me, can't you? How about taking me on your rounds?"

Charlotte looked unsure.

"I promise to uphold the spy code of honor," said Stacey solemnly, raising her right hand.

Charlotte giggled. "Okay," she agreed. "Let's go."

"What about a snack first?" asked Stacey. "Like, say, a nice tomato sandwich?" In the book, that's Harriet's favorite food.

Charlotte crinkled her nose. "Yuck," she said. "Can I just have some Fig Newtons instead?"

A few minutes later, Charlotte and Stacey were on their way. Charlotte's sweatshirt pocket was bulging with Fig Newtons, and her flashlight dangled from her belt. She carried a small backpack containing the tape recorder, a pair of binoculars (toy ones that weren't very high-powered, as far as Stacey could tell), and a pair of sunglasses ("my disguise," explained Charlotte).

"Okay," said Charlotte, all seriousness.

"Ready? Follow me." She led the way across the Johanssens' side yard. She stopped at the edge of the yard and positioned herself behind a large tree. She pointed to an overgrown bush nearby and motioned to Stacey to hide behind it. Then she pointed to a nearby house — which happens to be the Ramseys'.

"I can tell you exactly what's going on over there without even looking," she whispered to Stacey. "Jessi's probably downstairs in the basement, practicing ballet. She does lots of stretches, and sometimes she does pirouettes and things, just like a real ballerina." She paused. Then she pointed to another window, on the first floor of the house. "Aunt Cecelia's in the kitchen, making dinner for everyone. She takes all afternoon to cook. She talks on the phone while she's doing it. Gab, gab, gab."

Stacey stifled a smile. "What about Becca? What's she usually doing?"

Charlotte looked a little embarrassed. "Well, we used to play together a lot in the afternoons. But lately I've been kind of busy. So Becca's mostly been reading and stuff. In her room. Sometimes Vanessa comes over."

Stacey nodded. She wondered how Becca felt about Charlotte's new hobby.

Charlotte pulled her binoculars and the tape recorder out of her backpack. She watched the house for awhile and then made some mumbled comments into the recorder. "Okay," she said finally. "Ready for the next stop?" She led the way to a house across the street, slinking along from tree to tree and then making a break for it when she hit the road.

Stacey followed, trying to copy Charlotte's movements. She told me later that she was wondering if it was wrong to encourage Charlotte's spying, but she couldn't help herself. She was actually having fun.

She ducked behind a toolshed, joining Charlotte, who was already focusing her binoculars on a fenced-in yard behind a tidy little white house. "I see that Cheryl is out today. I guess that means they found her yesterday. She ran away for awhile." She swept the binoculars across the yard. "And Pooh Bear's out too. And Jacques. The whole crew."

Stacey laughed. "If I didn't know we were at the Mancusis' house, I'd really be wondering," she said. As it was, she knew Charlotte was talking about three dogs: a Great Dane, a poodle, and a golden retriever. The Mancusis are animal lovers. The BSC has done some pet-sitting for them now and then. Once, when Dawn was pet-sitting at their house, Cheryl, the Great Dane, disappeared for more than an afternoon. It turned out that she'd been dognapped, but Dawn and the rest of us went into detective mode and helped to catch the man who'd done it. The Mancusis have always been grateful.

"Do they have any new pets over there?" I asked Charlotte.

She nodded. "Remember Frank?" she asked. "The talking bird? Well, they found him a girl-friend. Her name's Annabelle, and she can sing 'Happy Birthday' in three languages."

"You're kidding," Stacey said.

She shook her head. "I even have it on tape," she said, holding up her recorder.

"You are quite the spy, Charlotte," said Stacey, laughing. She couldn't help being im-pressed. Charlotte took her all over the neigh-borhood that afternoon and shared the latest information on everyone in the area.

But Stacey was a little worried too. She didn't like hearing that Charlotte had stopped play-ing with Becca in the afternoons. And she was concerned that Charlotte might be caught one day. So far, she wasn't doing anything terribly wrong. But Stacey knew the situation could turn messy in a second if Charlotte wasn't careful.

CHAPTER 5

"Well, if it isn't Detective Thomas!"

I looked up to see Sergeant Winters standing over me. Officer Hopkins was standing next to him. Both of them were smiling. Sergeant Johnson was nowhere in sight. "Um, hi," I said. I was sitting in the waiting area at the Stoneybrook police station. It was Thursday afternoon, and I hadn't forgotten my appointment with Sergeant Johnson.

"Sergeant Johnson tells us you're quite the investigator," said Sergeant Winters. "He says you and your friends have helped to solve some of Stoneybrook's toughest mysteries."

"Well," I began, not knowing exactly what to say, "I guess —"

"Don't be modest," said Officer Hopkins. "Sergeant Johnson thinks you're terrific."

"Thanks," I said. "I like him too."

"We all do," said Sergeant Winters in a hearty voice. Then he dropped his voice down to a more confidential tone. "Tell me, Kristy," he said. "What time was it again when you first approached the Golem mansion?"

Was I being questioned? I looked around for Sergeant Johnson. I'd expected a real interview, in one of the questioning rooms. It was kind of odd to start in the waiting room. "Um, I guess it was around seven o'clock," I said.

"And you saw Sergeant Johnson responding to the alarm — when?" asked Officer Hopkins. She had pulled out a notebook, and she looked at me eagerly.

"I don't know, exactly," I said. "It was pretty soon after those alarms went off."

"How soon?" she asked, pen poised above the paper. "A matter of minutes? Seconds?"

"Maybe a couple of minutes." Why were they so interested in Sergeant Johnson's appearance? What did that have to do with the crime?

Sergeant Winters stroked his chin. "Now, how do you suppose he arrived there so quickly?" he asked, looking off into the distance.

It wasn't a real question. Which was a good thing, because I didn't know how to answer it. Anyway, just then Sergeant Johnson walked into the waiting room. He gave a quick glance at Officer Hopkins and Sergeant Winters. They nodded at him and then seemed to remember other business they had to take care of. Both of them disappeared in a hurry.

Sergeant Johnson ushered me into his office and closed the door. I'd barely sat down in the uncomfortable orange plastic chair he offered me before he asked me what Sergeant Winters and Officer Hopkins had wanted.

I felt awkward, since they'd been asking about him. "They just had some questions," I said. "About timing and stuff. When I first saw you, for example."

Sergeant Johnson raised his eyebrows, then shook his head. "Sergeant Winters is out of line. He has his nose in business where it doesn't belong." He sighed. "Winters came here from some big city," he said. "We haven't learned much about him except this: He knows the chief here is retiring soon, and he figures he might have a crack at taking over the job. Have you heard the expression 'A big frog in a little pond'? It means that it's easier to be a big shot in a small town like Stoneybrook." He paused. "That is one ambitious police officer. He won't stop until he's on top." He shook his head in disgust. "Well, anyway," he said, pulling a clipboard out of his drawer, "why don't we begin our interview?"

I looked around. "Here?" I asked.

He nodded. "Sometimes I use the questioning rooms, but for real privacy, my office is best. Nobody can overhear us here. Anyway, I'm not formally questioning you. If I was, your parents would have to be present. This is just a — consultation."

I shrugged. "Okay," I said.

Sergeant Johnson looked down at his desk. As usual, it was messy. I'd never seen it neat. He was probably working on about six cases at once. Files and pens and stacks of paper covered the entire surface. He cleared a spot and set the clipboard down. "Now," he began. "Let's just go through your whole story, beginning with why you were in the vicinity of the Golem residence." He looked at me expectantly. His pen was poised above the clean, blank form on his clipboard.

I took a deep breath. "Well," I said, "it all started when we decided to play hide-and-seek." I told him about our game and mentioned that Cary had snuck up on me. Then I told him that Karen had said she was more interested in exploring than in playing, so we'd begun to walk toward the mansion.

"Were you on the road at that point?" he asked. He was looking down at his clipboard, writing busily, so he didn't see my face light up.

"Yes!" I said, suddenly remembering something. "And you drove right past us, without even waving."

"I did?" he asked, looking up with a frown.

I nodded. "I forgot about that. How come you were all the way out there? That was before the alarm went off. Wasn't it?"

"Hey, who's doing the questioning here?" asked Sergeant Johnson, laughing a little. "I'm sorry I didn't wave to you. I guess I was pretty focused on what I was doing. I was answering another call out that way. Just a coincidence." He gave a little shrug.

"Oh." His explanation seemed simple enough, but I couldn't help thinking it was a little strange that the police were in the area *before* the crime even occurred. Clearly, though, he didn't want to talk about it any further.

"Tell me more about this Cary Retlin," said Sergeant Johnson.

"He's just a guy from school. He said he was bird-watching. He had binoculars with him, and a bird book." I didn't want to give out any more information on Cary than I had to. He was a troublemaker but that didn't make him a criminal.

"Was that the only time you saw him that day?" asked Sergeant Johnson.

"Well, no. I also saw him when you were talking to Sergeant Winters about the Cat Burglar. I think he heard all the sirens and came over to check out what was going on. But when I looked at him, he ducked behind a toolshed." I was trying to be honest. Unfortunately, it made Cary sound, well, suspicious. "But I really don't think he had anything to do with the burglary," I said hastily. "I think he was just curious."

"I see," said Sergeant Johnson. He made a few more notes. "And did you see anyone else in the woods? Anybody at all?"

"Nobody," I replied, shaking my head. "Just David Michael and Karen — and you."

"You didn't see the security guard drive away, did you?"

I told him I didn't remember seeing any cars other than police cars.

"What about this man?" asked Sergeant Johnson. He leaned forward to pull a picture out of a file on his desk. Then he stood up and brought it around to show me. It was a Polaroid snapshot of a youngish guy (older than Charlie, but way younger than Watson) with brown hair and a goatee.

"Nope," I said, shaking my head. "Who is he, anyway? The Cat Burglar?"

Sergeant Johnson shook his head. "This is Ben Birch. He's a business associate of Reinhart Golem. I'm wondering if he might be mixed up with this in some way."

"Well, I didn't see him," I said.

Sergeant Johnson stepped over to a desktop copier and made a copy of the picture. "Why don't you hang on to this," he said, "just in case you remember something." He gave me the copy. I took it, even though I knew I hadn't seen the guy and therefore would never remember anything about him.

We talked awhile longer. Sergeant Johnson took down everything I told him about hearing what I thought was a gunshot, then hearing the alarm go off and seeing the lights and being scared out of my wits when he ran up behind David Michael and Karen and me.

"Sorry about that," he said. "I was just concerned for your safety. I didn't know then that the Cat Burglar was responsible. He may be devious, but he's never hurt anyone. It's not his style."

I was dying to ask more about the Cat Burglar, but I knew Sergeant Johnson couldn't tell me much in the middle of an investigation. The BSC members could do some research and find out more. So I kept my questions simple. "Does he always leave the sign of the cat?" I asked. Secretly I thought that cat sign was way cool, even though the guy was a criminal.

Sergeant Johnson nodded. "It's his calling card," he said. "It's almost like a taunt. He revels in his ability to work around the most sophisticated security systems. Like Golem's. There are three levels to that system, and it would have been almost impossible to avoid tripping the alarm. But he figured out how to do most of his work first, before he set off the motion sensors. That gave him time to clear out before the law arrived."

Sergeant Johnson seemed to have quite a grasp on how the Cat Burglar had carried out his most recent crime. He'd been doing his homework, all right.

"Do you know for sure what was stolen?" I asked, remembering what the security guard had said about diamonds.

"That hasn't been established yet," said Sergeant Johnson. "There was a vault in the mansion, and it did appear to have been opened forcibly. Mr. Fenton says he was told it contained diamonds, but there are no diamonds in there now. It seems as if they were stolen, but so far the evidence is circumstantial. I haven't been able to reach Reinhart Golem yet to discuss the case with him."

"Where is he?" I asked.

"According to the security company, he's at his summer home in France. He always lets them know his travel plans. They say he's due back soon. I've been calling him regularly, with no luck." Just then the phone rang. Sergeant Johnson answered it, spoke a few terse words, then hung up. He pushed back his chair and sighed. "I guess that's all we have time for today, Kristy," he said. "Thanks for coming in. I'll be in touch if any more questions come up." He stood to shake my hand. "I know you and your friends will be wanting to play detective," he said. "You can't keep the BSC away from a mystery like this one. But be careful, all right? Don't forget that there may be a gun involved. And come to me if you find out anything interesting. Deal?"

"Deal," I said, shaking his hand. It was hard not to feel a little thrill of excitement. There was no question about it. I had stumbled into a first-class mystery. And with any luck, the BSC would be able to help solve it.

CHAPTER
6

"So, how did it go?" Mary Anne stood up to greet me as I walked back into the waiting room from Sergeant Johnson's office.

"Are you a suspect?" asked Claudia, grinning.

I was glad to see my friends. I wanted to tell them everything Sergeant Johnson had said about the Cat Burglar, before I forgot any of it. But just as I was about to answer, I was interrupted.

"Can't a guy watch birds in peace?"

It was Cary Retlin. He and his dad emerged from one of the questioning rooms, where, I figured, Cary had just had his interview with Sergeant Winters and Officer Hopkins, and walked down the hall toward us. His dad left, saying he had to go back to work. But Cary joined us, complaining loudly. "I mean, come on, it's not as if *I* stole any diamonds. What would I do with diamonds?"

"I'm sure they don't really consider you a suspect," Mary Anne said soothingly.

"Oh, no?" asked Cary, arching an eyebrow. "Then why did I have to answer thirty gazillion questions about where, when, and why I was in the woods that day? Don't they have anything better to do than bother me?" He looked irritated. "I mean, they have more information than they're letting on. They should leave me alone and focus on what's really going on."

"What do you mean?" I asked. I had the strangest feeling that Cary knew something I didn't know.

"Oh, nothing," he said, waving a hand in disgust. "I'm tired of wasting my time here. Let's go." He turned on his heel and left the building.

I looked at Mary Anne and Claudia. We all shrugged. Then we followed Cary.

He was waiting for us on the sidewalk.

"So, want to head over there?" he asked.

"Where?" I was confused.

"To the Golem place," he said, as if it were obvious. "The scene of the crime."

"But —"

"But what? Are you scared?"

"No!" I cried.

"Kristy's never scared," Mary Anne said.

"And we're not either," said Claudia.

"It's just that, in this case," I began, trying to figure out what to say, "maybe we should leave things up to the police. Until they're a little further along in their investigation, that is." It wasn't that I didn't want to solve the mystery. I just wasn't so eager to go back to that spooky house. Especially when I still didn't know what that gunshot had been about. It didn't seem safe. I thought it might make more sense to do some other, less dangerous investigating first. "I thought maybe I'd spend some time at the library today," I said. "You know, reading up on the Cat Burglar and stuff."

Cary gave me an exasperated look. "Okay, first of all — bor-ing. Why go to the library when you could be checking out a cool mansion? And second — leaving this one up to the police might not be the wisest thing."

"Why do you say that?" I asked.

But he brushed my question aside. "Come on, are you in or are you in?"

"We're in," said Claudia, stepping forward. Mary Anne, I noticed, did not step forward with her. In fact, Mary Anne just stood there, looking nervous. I didn't say anything. "Come on," Claudia urged us. "I haven't even had the chance to see this place yet. Let's go take a little peek. What's the harm?"

"That's the spirit," said Cary. He took her arm and walked off down the sidewalk, toward the rack where we'd left our bikes. Once again, Mary Anne and I looked at each other, shrugged, and fell into step behind Cary.

We hopped on our bikes, fastened our helmets, and rode off down the street. Toward trouble? I didn't know. But I had butterflies in my stomach, and they seemed to multiply as we drew closer to the Golem mansion. By the time we were riding down the quiet, tree-lined private road, the butterflies were fluttering like mad. In fact, I was so preoccupied with my own nerves that I almost didn't hear Cary's warning call of "Car!" Still, I was able to swerve out of the way in time to let the car — a police cruiser — go by. It seemed to be coming from the Golem mansion.

"Was that Sergeant Winters?" I asked Claudia after the car had passed.

She shrugged. "I don't know the guy," she said. "But from your description, it sure looked like him."

He must have raced out there after his interview with Cary. I wondered why. But soon I forgot about him, because we were turning into the driveway of the mansion, passing the huge stone gate.

We stopped for a moment by the entrance while I pointed out the mailbox to Claudia and Mary Anne. "See? There's the cat symbol," I said.

Claudia traced it with her finger. "A stencil. It looks as if he used one of those permanent markers." I could tell she thought it was cool too.

"Is it always red?" Mary Anne wanted to know.

I shrugged. "I don't know. I think so. Sergeant Johnson seemed to think it was."

Cary raised that eyebrow. "I think we need to forget everything the police told us and concentrate on finding our own clues," he said. "Come on, let's go check the place out."

We stowed our bikes behind the gatehouse, and Cary led us down the drive, right to the mansion. He approached one of the oversize, old-fashioned windows, pushed back some ivy that was hanging over it, and peered in.

"The drawing room," he said. "Can you believe this place has a drawing room? Plus two living rooms, a parlor, a huge kitchen, a gym and spa — *with* sauna — and about ten bedrooms, all upstairs." He paused, thinking. "It's weird. I seem to remember seeing a light on in one of them the day of the burglary."

How did Cary know so much about the house? Could he have figured all of that out just by peeking into the windows? I narrowed my eyes and stared at him. Was it possible that he — ? Then I shook my head. No way was Cary the Cat Burglar. As he'd said, what would a kid his age do with a bunch of diamonds?

I stepped up to look into the window. The room inside looked kind of eerie. All the furniture was covered with white cloths. A white cloth even hung over what I guessed was a huge painting above the cavernous fireplace. And on either side of the painting white cloths covered what had to be — I shuddered a little — animal heads, judging by the shape. "Ew," I said.

Cary heard me. "I think he's into big game hunting," he said. "Gross, huh?"

I nodded. We moved to another window, which Claudia and Mary Anne were already peering into.

"It's the gym," said Claudia.

"Or else a torture room," said Mary Anne. Her eyes were big and round when she looked back at me.

I had to check this out for myself. Sure enough, the room looked like a gym, sort of. I couldn't identify all the equipment. Some of it looked familiar, but some of it was downright bizarre. One device looked as if it were meant for stretching you out while hanging you from your ankles. Um, no thanks.

"So, let's look for bullet casings," said Cary, turning from the window.

"What?" asked Mary Anne.

"Kristy heard a gunshot, right?" asked Cary.

"Or at least she thought she did. If it was a gun, there ought to be a bullet casing around. That's what's left after a gun goes off."

Cary had a point. If we could find some physical evidence, I'd know for sure that I'd heard a gunshot. We spread out to look, walking around the house.

We poked through the garden beds, searched in the ivy that sprawled all over the house. We looked over the front steps (they were grand, carved out of marble) and checked the side entrance (not so grand — originally it must have been meant for servants). Finally, I checked out the back porch while Cary did a search of the garage and Mary Anne and Claudia continued around the house.

That's when I saw it. A flash of gold. "Hey!" I yelled as I bent to take a closer look. "Check out what I found!" Cary came running, with Mary Anne and Claudia right behind him. "Anybody have a tissue?" I asked. Mary Anne gave me a strange look, but rummaged around in her backpack until she found one. She handed it over and I used it to pick up the object. "Don't want to disturb any fingerprints," I explained. I showed Cary the item I'd found: a small, hollow, brass cylinder with a flat base.

"Good going," Cary said, thumping me on the back. "It's a bullet casing, all right."

I was glad he knew. I hadn't been sure.

"I wonder if there's a bullet hole that goes with this," Cary mused. He looked around.

"Is that one?" asked Mary Anne, pointing to a spot on the porch door.

"You bet," said Cary, reaching up to finger it. It was a perfect little hole, like the kind a drill makes.

"Wow," breathed Claudia.

"And look what I found," said Mary Anne. She held up a red object. She'd used another tissue to pick it up by the tip.

"A Magic Marker!" Cary exclaimed. "Yes!" He pumped a fist in the air. "That must be the one he used to leave his mark on the mailbox. This is awesome. We're finding clues right and left."

I had to admit it was pretty exciting, though for a second I wondered why the police hadn't found those things if they'd done such a thorough search. Anyway, we hunted for another half hour or so and found nothing more.

"I should head home soon," said Claudia finally.

"Me too," agreed Mary Anne.

I was ready to give up for the day myself. But Cary was still peering into windows. "Oh, let's just take one more look," I said. It was impossible to resist. Let this be a warning: Once you start snooping, it can be hard to stop.

I headed for a window I hadn't checked before and leaned into it, shading my eyes with my hands in order to get a good look inside.

"AAAUGHHH!" I cried, jumping away from the window.

"What is it?" asked Mary Anne, rushing to me.

I was too scared to speak. Why?

Because somebody was in that room. And he was staring right back at me.

CHAPTER 7

"Kristy! Are you okay?" Claudia ran to me too. Cary was right behind her.

I still couldn't speak. Instead, I just pointed toward the window. Claudia took one look and her face went white. "Oh. My. Lord," she said.

Mary Anne had seen the face too. She gripped my hand. "What should we do?" she whispered in a tense voice. "Do you think we should run for it?"

I sensed that she was about to panic. I could hardly blame her. But, for the moment, running was out of the question. I was paralyzed.

Just then, Cary did something that convinced me once and for all that he is completely and totally nuts. He looked up at the window and with a big grin on his face, waved at the person staring back at us.

"Cary!" I hissed. "What are you —"

"Oh my lord," Claudia breathed again. She pointed to the window. The person — I could now see that it was a man with a blond mustache — was grinning and waving back.

This was too weird.

Then the person pointed toward the back door in an unmistakable gesture that meant he'd meet us there. I looked at Cary. If he was scared, he didn't show it. In fact, he was still grinning. And without a pause, he headed for the back door.

"Welcome, welcome," said the man, who met us on the porch steps. "So nice to see some local kids around. You are local, aren't you? I'm afraid I haven't met many of my neighbors, since I'm hardly ever here. You've come right on time — I just got back from France an hour ago."

He was acting as if he were the owner of the house. Could it be true? Could this man be Reinhart Golem?

"Allow me to introduce myself," he said just then, and bowed slightly. "I'm Reinhart Golem," he said. "And this is my home."

There was something very, very strange about Reinhart Golem. First of all, he didn't seem at all annoyed to find a bunch of kids snooping around his house. Second, even though I was staring at him, I found it hard to figure out the most basic things about him — for example, how old he was. At first I thought he was in his twenties. Then, when he turned his face a certain way, I could have sworn he looked much older, closer to Watson's age. And again, when he looked straight at me, for just an instant he could have been a teenager. It was eerie.

What did he look like? Well, he was tall and slim, and he had wavy, dark blond hair, not too long, but not too short either. His eyes were green, or were they gray? I couldn't be sure. They seemed to change all the time. He was dressed in what looked like very expensive clothes. Stacey could probably have told you which Italian designer had created his perfectly tailored shirt and pants, both of which were black. Golem looked familiar somehow, but I couldn't put my finger on why. Maybe he reminded me of some old-time movie star.

"Please, have a seat," he said, gesturing around the porch. He had nicer furniture out there than most people have in their living rooms: wicker chairs with plump cushions, a huge couch that two people could have slept on comfortably, a hammock just made for lazy afternoon naps.

I sat on the couch, and Mary Anne sat down beside me. Cary and Claudia each chose chairs. Reinhart Golem didn't sit. Instead, he leaned against the wall or strolled around with his hands in his pockets as we talked. It was as if sitting still didn't suit him, as if he needed to be on the move all the time.

He asked us our names, and we told him. Then he asked what we were doing there at his house. He didn't seem mad — just curious. Something about the way he asked made me feel it was fine to be honest with him. I looked around at the others and I could see that they felt the same way.

"We were investigating," I said.

He cocked his head.

"You know, the burglary," I went on. "We were just looking around for clues."

"And did you find any?" he asked with a little smile.

"As a matter of fact, we did," I said. I dug into my pocket and pulled out the tissue-wrapped bullet casing. "I found this. Right outside, on the stairs. And there's a bullet hole too." Then Mary Anne showed him the Magic Marker she'd found.

"Fascinating," said Golem. He walked over to me and examined the casing for a moment. "We'll have to call Sergeant Winters immediately," he said. "He was here only recently, asking some questions. No doubt he'll want to come back and take a look at this. Excuse me, will you?" he asked. Then he glided off into the house, and I wondered why Sergeant Winters had been the one to question Golem. Golem came back a few moments later and said the police were on their way.

"While we wait, why don't you tell me a little more about your investigation. Is this the first time you've tried your hand at detective work?"

"Oh, no," said Mary Anne. Then she blushed and fell silent. I could tell she felt too shy to go on, so I jumped in.

"We belong to a club," I explained. "At least, the three of us do," I said, pointing to myself, Claudia, and Mary Anne. "It's a baby-sitting club, but we've been doing detective work for a long time. We've helped solve some major cases here in Stoneybrook, and in other places too."

Golem looked impressed. And intrigued. "What sort of criminals have you caught?" he asked.

"Oh, you know," I said, trying to sound casual. "Counterfeiters, dognappers, jewel thieves —"

"Jewel thieves?" asked Golem.

"Uh-huh," said Claudia.

I glanced at Cary. He was looking impressed. I bet he didn't know the BSC did more than take care of kids.

Golem spoke again. "Perhaps you could help me," he said slowly. "As you may know, some valuable diamonds were stolen from a vault in this house during the break-in."

So it was true. Suddenly, my heart was beating a little faster. The diamonds really were missing. And their owner wanted our help! It was so cool that he took us seriously. Weird, too, in a way. I mean, why was he talking to us so freely? After all, we're just a bunch of kids. Most adults would expect the police to handle a crime like this. But I didn't care. I was too interested in the mystery.

"Do you have any idea who took them?" I asked. "Could it have been Ben Birch?" In my eagerness, I jumped right in and spoke without thinking.

Golem gave me a sharp look. His face suddenly looked pale. "Ben Birch?" he asked. "How — and *what* — do you know about Ben Birch?"

Oops. I'd said something that hadn't pleased him. "I, um, I don't know," I said. "I guess it was just a name I heard. I don't know anything about him."

"Mr. Birch is a former business associate of mine," said Golem. "I bought him out years ago, long before my business prospered. He may not be happy about that. He may even carry a small grudge. But if you think that he would stoop to robbing my home, well, that is a most unlikely scenario."

"Okay," I said in a small voice. I was embarrassed but determined not to let my misstep ruin our chances of helping out with the investigation.

Mary Anne sensed my discomfort. "Do you have any other ideas about suspects?" she asked Golem.

I shot her a grateful look.

"I suppose my security guard would have to be considered a suspect," he said. "Now that I think about it, he may not be as loyal to me as I would have hoped. Just because someone wears a uniform doesn't mean he's trustworthy. And then there's this Cat Burglar character, of course." Just then, we heard a car in the drive. "That must be Sergeant Winters," he said.

Moments later, Sergeant Winters and Officer Hopkins appeared on the porch steps. Golem invited them to sit down. He made sure that everyone was acquainted. Then he showed them the bullet casing and the Magic Marker. He was a little careless about handling them — I wondered if he might have ruined our chance for clear fingerprints.

"Well, would you look at that," said Sergeant Winters.

"Nice work," said Officer Hopkins. "Those are important pieces of evidence." She put both of them into a plastic bag.

"I found it hard to believe that kids so young could be such good detectives," admitted Sergeant Winters. "But I guess Sergeant Johnson was right."

I was glowing. So were Claudia and Mary Anne. But when Sergeant Winters and Officer Hopkins followed Golem outside to look at the spot where I'd found the casing, Cary caught my eye.

"Don't let it go to your head," he said, looking skeptical.

Was he jealous? I decided to ignore him. When Sergeant Winters and Officer Hopkins returned, they still looked impressed. For the moment, that was all I cared about.

Sergeant Winters sat down next to me, and Officer Hopkins took a nearby chair. The others on the porch were still talking about the big clues we'd found, but Sergeant Winters seemed to have other things on his mind. He began to question me quietly, asking about Sergeant Johnson's role the day of the burglary. When he asked me again when I'd first seen Sergeant Johnson, I told him that I'd remembered some new information. I explained that Sergeant Johnson had driven past us on the road just minutes before the alarm had gone off.

Sergeant Winters listened, shooting occasional glances at Officer Hopkins, as if to say, "See what I meant?" Finally, after he'd grilled me for several minutes, he excused himself and asked Golem if he could use his phone to call the station. "You'll have to show me where it is," he said to Golem. "Sergeant Johnson might know his way around this house, but I don't." Golem led him into the house. "Chief will want to know about this," I heard Sergeant Winters mumble to Officer Hopkins as he passed her.

"Why would Sergeant Johnson know his way around?" I asked Officer Hopkins.

"He had a search warrant for this place some time ago," she answered. "A different case." She waved a hand dismissively.

When Sergeant Winters came back, he sat down beside me again. "Kristy, I want you to do me a big favor."

"Sure," I said, bewildered. What could he have in mind?

"Don't talk about this case with Sergeant Johnson anymore."

"What?" I asked. "Why not?" Then I realized that Sergeant Winters must believe that Sergeant Johnson had done something wrong.

He shook his head. "I can't answer that. But this is important. Will you promise me?"

I paused. "Is he a suspect?" I asked finally. I couldn't understand how he could be, but why else would I be forbidden to talk to him? I thought fast, trying to put the pieces together. True, Sergeant Johnson had been in the area at the time of the crime. And I had to admit he had been acting odd lately. But still — Sergeant Johnson? I didn't know anyone more trustworthy. Anyway, wasn't this job the work of the Cat Burglar? Or was it the work of someone *pretending* to be the Cat Burglar. A *copy*cat burglar? My head was spinning.

Sergeant Winters wouldn't answer. I thought privately that he was acting a little suspicious himself.

"I think we've covered enough ground for today," said Sergeant Winters finally. He must have seen that I wasn't ready to promise not to talk to Sergeant Johnson. "How would you kids like a ride home?"

"We have our bikes," said Claudia.

"You can leave them in the garage for now," offered Golem.

That was tempting. It meant we'd have an excuse to come back. I was about to accept when Cary spoke up.

"We'd just as soon ride," he said, shooting me a glance that said *don't argue*.

"Fine," said Officer Hopkins. She and Sergeant Winters headed out the door.

As we started to follow them, Golem pulled a white rectangle out of his pocket. "Let me give you my card," he said. "This has all my addresses on it; here in Stoneybrook, as well as in New York and in France. Keep in touch, won't you? If you can help me track down those diamonds you'll be handsomely rewarded."

A reward! Claudia and I exchanged an excited glance.

I took the card. "We'll call if we figure anything out," I promised. I dug into my pocket and pulled out a wrinkled, torn BSC flier I'd been carrying around. "Here's where you can reach us," I said, giving it to him.

"Let's *go*," Cary hissed in my ear. He seemed nervous. He raced us through our good-byes to Golem, then led us down the drive to our bikes. Finally, when we were riding along the road, I asked him what was up.

"You may not know much about guns," he began, "but I do. And I took a good look at the ones in the holsters those police officers were wearing."

"Yes?" I asked.

"That bullet casing — it came from the same type of automatic pistol."

Whoa. My brain clicked along quickly. If I could trust Cary's words — a big "if" — this was important news. No doubt Sergeant Johnson carried the same type of gun as Officer Hopkins and Sergeant Winters. Was it possible? *Could* Sergeant Johnson be the thief?

CHAPTER 8

"How *big* a reward? Are we talking thousands?" Jessi was excited.

"Even hundreds would be cool," said Abby.

"We'd do our best to solve this mystery even if there wasn't a reward," Stacey added. "But the money sure wouldn't hurt. Now, how are we going to find out more about the Cat Burglar?"

It was Friday, BSC meeting time. Only we weren't paying much attention to BSC business. I'd decided that the mystery of the Cat Burglar deserved center stage. We were going to spend the entire meeting discussing it. Sure, we'd answer the phone when it rang, but that was it. Meanwhile, it was time to go over everything we knew and start thinking in terms of suspects, clues, and leads.

In fact, Mary Anne had even brought out the mystery notebook. It contains every scrap of information about recent mysteries we've investigated. (It's a much neater way to keep track of things than our original system, which consisted mostly of saving things like pizza napkins and math worksheets on which we'd jotted down clues.) Mary Anne had already started a section for this mystery.

Claudia, Mary Anne, and I had filled the others in on my meeting with Sergeant Johnson, our discovery of two important pieces of evidence, and our introduction to Reinhart Golem. Most important, they knew about the reward.

Mallory spoke up. "I have some information," she said. "I was at the library last night and I couldn't resist spending some time researching the Cat Burglar."

"Excellent!" I said. "Tell us everything you learned."

"Okay, but it isn't a lot. He's a pretty mysterious character."

"How do you know it's a he?" Jessi interrupted.

Mal smiled. "Good point," she said. "I suppose it's possible that this Cat is female. I never really thought about it. Okay, so maybe it's a woman. But I'm still going to say 'he,' since that's how all the articles referred to the person."

"So, how long has he been around?" I asked.

"At least a couple of years," answered Mal.

"He's worked all over the East Coast. He doesn't pull a lot of jobs, but the ones he does pull are big. Then he tends to lie low for awhile. I guess if you steal two million dollars worth of gold from someone's private safe, you have enough to live on for a while. Even if your tastes run to heavy cream and the finest, freshest fish. It sounds as if this Cat enjoys a luxurious life." She giggled.

"Two million dollars worth of gold?" repeated Stacey. "That *is* a huge heist."

"I know," said Mal. "That was from a wealthy New Yorker, somebody who lived on Central Park West. But it wasn't the Cat Burglar's biggest job. He's stolen jewels, antiques, all kinds of things. Once he even stole a very rare blue Tiffany lamp from an Italian prince. There's no way he could sell a thing like that; the police would be all over him in a second. So he must have stolen it for himself. He definitely seems to enjoy nice things."

"Well, Golem has nice things," I said. "I can see why he'd be a target for the Cat Burglar."

"Or for a copycat," Mary Anne reminded me. "Somebody else could have left that stencil of a cat. Somebody who was just pretending to be the Cat Burglar."

"True," I said. "So, if that's the case, who would our suspects be?"

"I really hate to say this," said Claudia, "but

isn't Sergeant Johnson kind of a suspect?"

We all fell silent. Everyone in the BSC looks up to Sergeant Johnson. It was hard even to think of considering him as a criminal. But the idea had already crossed my mind. We had to admit that there was something suspicious about the way he'd been acting. And Sergeant Winters and Officer Hopkins seemed to agree.

"It's possible," I admitted reluctantly. "He could have broken in and stolen the diamonds. Maybe he set off the alarm on purpose just to make it look like a real robbery. He seems to know all about that alarm system. And *maybe* he could have made it out of there just in time to act as if he was responding to the alarm."

We were all silent again. Nobody really wanted to believe it, least of all me.

"What about that security guard?" asked Stacey finally. "Has anybody checked out his story? He said he had an emergency phone call, but who knows if that was true? He could have stolen the diamonds and then rigged the alarm to go off when he was away."

"And Cary — I thought he was acting a little suspicious," put in Claudia. "Doesn't it seem as if he knows more than he's letting on? And how does he know so much about guns and bullets and all that, anyway?"

"I just thought of someone else!" I said.

"This guy Ben Birch. Golem said he wouldn't have done it, but who knows? Since he and Golem worked together, he might have had inside information about the diamonds, and if he was mad enough at Golem after they broke up their business relationship, he might have decided to steal them."

Mary Anne was taking notes as we talked. "This is quite a list of suspects," she said. "Obviously, we're going to have to do a lot more investigating."

Just then, the phone rang. I put down the Milky Way bar I'd been about to bite into (Claudia had provided great munchies, as always) and answered the call. "Baby-sitters Club," I said. I heard a chuckle on the other end.

"I'm not actually looking for a sitter," said Golem. I knew it was him the second I heard his voice. "This is Reinhart Golem, and what I'm looking for is a detective."

I didn't skip a beat. "Well, you've called the right place," I said. "How can I help you?" I wished with all my might that Claudia's phone had a speaker option, so everyone else could hear this call. I mouthed his name so that they would know who I was talking to.

"You can help by telling me more about this Sergeant Johnson I've been hearing about," he said. "Tell me, do you know the man?"

My heart skipped a beat. "Sure. We've worked with him before."

"And you find him trustworthy?"

I paused. What was I supposed to say? It didn't feel right to admit my suspicions to a stranger. I didn't even want to admit them to myself. "I always have in the past," I said carefully. "He's a good police officer and a friend."

"A friend? Hmm. Well, you may be interested to know that it looks as if your 'friend's' fingerprints may have been all over that red Magic Marker you discovered at my house yesterday."

My stomach flip-flopped. "I'm sure there's an explanation for that if it's true," I said.

"Certainly," said Golem. "I'm sure everything will be explained soon enough. And I have the sense that you and your friends will be the ones to put it all together. You strike me as very clever young people."

I couldn't help being flattered. Reinhart Golem was a strange guy, but I liked the way he gave us credit for being more than just kids. "Well, thanks," I said, feeling awkward.

"No, thank *you*. Do you still have my card, in case you think of anything you'd like to tell me?"

I checked my back pocket. Fortunately, I was wearing the same jeans I'd worn the day before. The card was right where I'd stuck it. "I do," I said.

"Very well, then," said Golem. "Don't forget about the reward. I'm sure we'll be in touch." He hung up.

Slowly, I hung up too. Then I faced my friends. "You won't believe what he just told me," I said. "He says Sergeant Johnson's fingerprints may be on that Magic Marker."

Mary Anne gasped.

I shook my head, looking down at the card in my hand. That's when I noticed something funny. "Hey, Mal," I said. "Where did you say that burglary took place? The one in New York?"

She checked her notes. "In an apartment building on Central Park West." She read me the address.

"Interesting," I said. "It looks as if Golem has an apartment in the same building. I wonder if the Cat Burglar has been planning to rob him for a long time. It would have made sense to scope out that apartment but to pull the heist out here, at his Stoneybrook house, so nobody would be suspicous."

"Except us," said Claudia proudly. "The BSC Detective Agency never misses a clue."

We talked for awhile longer and ended up deciding that what we really needed to do was hunt for more clues. We agreed to split up and follow some leads, making sure to write up any discoveries in the mystery notebook. Mal, Claudia, and Abby all made entries the very next day.

Saturday

More on the Cat Burglar: I spent all morning at the library, reading through accounts of his other burglaries and trying to find any other coincidences like the one with Reinhart Golem's New York address. Not much came up, except that I did read about one other burglary, and the policeman interviewed was named Officer Johnson. Could it be our Sergeant Johnson?

Saturday

I was at the library too. Trying to find out infourmation about Ben Birch. And heres' the weerd thing: I culdn't find a thing. There was nothing about him anywhare. Not even in any of the articals about Reinhart Golem. So what kind of buisness partner was he, anyway?

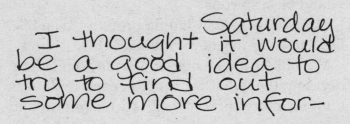

Saturday

I thought it would be a good idea to try to find out some more information about Jack Fenton, the security guard. I tracked down the company he works for. It's called Maximum security. The address was in the phone book. I rode my bike by today and learned that they operate out of a storefront on the edge of town.

Then I went home and made some calls, pretending I was a homeowner. I asked if all the guards had perfectly clean records. The lady who answered the phone wouldn't give me a straight answer! I think we need to check this guy out some more. He would have been in a perfect position to steal the diamonds!

CHAPTER 9

Sunday

Okay, I hearby announce that this spy game is officialy out of controle. I mean, its one thing for one of our charges to spy on her nieghbors. Its another thing when everybody is doing it. And now for the last straw! You wont believe who Charlotte spied on today.

I couldn't blame Claudia for being a tiny bit bent out of shape. I would have been too. . . .

Claudia arrived at the Johanssens' on Sunday afternoon. She was looking forward to her sitting job, since she'd read Stacey's notes in the club notebook. Claudia thought the *Harriet the Spy* game was great. It's one of her favorite books, and she's always admired Harriet. So it was fine with her that Charlotte wanted to spy. Claudia thought it would be fun to join Charlotte on her "rounds." She'd even dressed for the occasion, in her version of the Harriet outfit. Claudia was wearing purple painter's pants with lots of loops and pockets for carrying tools, red high-tops with purple laces, and a red sweatshirt customized with purple embroidery. She was even wearing glasses like Harriet's (with plain lenses since Claudia's eyesight is fine), but the frames were purple instead of black. Claudia was all set.

What she didn't bargain for was the fact that Charlotte wasn't the only spy in the neighborhood anymore.

Far from it.

In fact, as it turned out, spy fever was spreading like wildfire.

That wasn't obvious right away, though. When Claudia and Charlotte started their rounds (it hadn't taken much convincing for

Charlotte to agree to company), their first stop was the Ramseys'. Charlotte was all set with her backpack full of spying tools, but as it turned out, they weren't needed. The Ramsey house was empty. Aunt Cecelia was out, and Jessi and her mom were out too. And Becca?

"That's funny," said Charlotte. "I thought Vanessa was coming over to play with Becca today."

"And why did you think that?" asked Claudia.

"Oh," said Charlotte, blushing a little, "just something I overheard."

Claudia nodded. So Charlotte was spying on her best friends now. "I see," she said. She didn't want to remind Charlotte to be careful. She knew Stacey had already done that, and she knew Charlotte was smart. No doubt she already understood the risks.

The next stop was the Mancusis'. Not much was happening there either, although Charlotte made some careful observations into her tape recorder about the fact that Pooh Bear was digging in the garden again. After that, Charlotte led the way to the Rodowskys' house. "This should be more interesting," she promised Claudia. "There's always something going on here."

Claudia laughed. "That's for sure," she said. She knows the three Rodowsky boys. My friends and I have a private nickname for Jackie, the middle boy. We call him the Walking Disaster, because he's so accident-prone. We love Jackie, but we're always prepared for the worst when we sit for him.

Sure enough, there was plenty of activity at the Rodowskys'. Claudia and Charlotte snuck up close to the house and hid behind a huge tree to watch. The boys were out in the driveway, playing basketball. Shea, the oldest, was acting like a radio announcer, calling every play as it happened. Jackie was dribbling wildly, and Archie, the youngest, waved his arms in an effort to guard Jackie.

But the scene on the driveway wasn't what caught Charlotte's eye. "Would you look at that?" she whispered as she stared through her binoculars at another big tree on the other side of the Rodowskys' yard.

"What?" whispered Claudia. Charlotte handed her the binoculars and Claudia took a look. Then she almost burst out laughing — but caught herself just in time and giggled quietly instead. What she'd seen was another group of spies keeping tabs on the Rodowsky boys. It was the Pike triplets, Mal's ten-year-old brothers. They were also dressed in spy clothes, including three sets of fake noses with glasses and mustaches attached. Each of them carried a notebook and pen, and they passed around a pair of binoculars as they watched Archie, Shea, and Jackie play.

"Have they spotted us?" Charlotte whispered.

Claudia shook her head. "I don't think so," she said under her breath.

"Then we'll spy on the spies," said Charlotte. She giggled softly. She asked for the binoculars again and sat watching for a few minutes. Then she pulled out her tape recorder and spoke quietly into it. "Adam is wearing one of Mallory's old T-shirts," she said. "He'd die if anyone knew it used to belong to a girl. And Jordan just picked his nose when he thought nobody was looking." She watched for a little while longer until she found something to say about the last triplet. "Byron needs a haircut," she reported. "That little place in back is sticking up and he keeps trying to flatten it down, but it doesn't work."

She shut off the recorder and motioned to Claudia. "Let's go before they see us," she said. She scurried away from the tree, and Claudia followed her.

"That was a riot!" she crowed as she led Claudia back to the Ramseys' to see if anyone had come home yet. "Watching those guys spy was even more fun than just regular spying."

"Shh!" said Claudia.

"What?" asked Charlotte.

"I think there are even more spies around," said Claudia, nodding toward Jessi's house. There, behind the same large bush Charlotte had used for a hiding place, were Matt and Haley Braddock. They were staring intently into the Ramseys' backyard, where Aunt Cecelia was talking to a man Claudia had never seen before.

"Do you think that's her new boyfriend?" asked Charlotte in a whisper.

"I don't know," said Claudia, who, as she told me later, was pretty curious herself. "Let's move in closer."

"But then Matt and Haley will see us!" said Charlotte.

"So let's join them," suggested Claudia. "Maybe they've already figured out who the guy is."

Charlotte was reluctant, but as they tiptoed closer, Matt turned around and saw them anyway. He gestured eagerly, waving them over.

"Hi," whispered Charlotte, when the four spies were squished in behind the bush. "What's going on?"

Haley answered, speaking softly. "First we thought it was a romance. But Matt read their lips and it turned out that he's just a landscaper. He's here to help her plan a new garden."

Charlotte grinned at Matt. He's profoundly

deaf and communicates mostly through American Sign Language, which Haley can translate. But he's also an excellent lip-reader. "Cool," said Charlotte. Claudia could tell that Charlotte was already planning to learn how to lip-read. What a great skill for a spy!

After they'd watched for awhile longer, Charlotte poked Claudia and whispered, "Becca and Vanessa still aren't here. Let's go. I want to head home and listen to my notes." Claudia nodded, and they said good-bye to Matt and Haley and headed back to the Johanssens'.

Charlotte settled in on the front porch with her tape recorder and started listening to the notes she'd whispered into it that day. Claudia listened too. "What are you going to do with those tapes?" she asked.

"Just save them, I guess," said Charlotte. "Someday, when I grow up and become a famous writer, I'll be able to listen to them and remember all the stuff that happened in my old neighborhood."

Just then, Claudia heard a soft sound, like a stifled giggle. "What was that?" she asked.

"I don't know," said Charlotte. She looked around. "Hey!" she said, suddenly jumping to her feet, hands on hips. "What do you think you're doing?"

Claudia stood up too and leaned over the porch railing to see what Charlotte was looking at. There were Vanessa and Becca, who were crouched behind a bush next to the house.

Vanessa stood up. "What does it look like we're doing? We're spying." At that, she and Becca broke into full-scale giggles.

"On *me*?" Charlotte looked outraged.

"Why not?" asked Becca. "You spy on me all the time!"

"It's not the same," cried Charlotte.

"Is too," said Vanessa.

"Anyway, I had to do something. You weren't playing with me anymore," said Becca.

"But —" Charlotte began.

Claudia saw that the girls were heading for a fight. "Hold on, hold on," she said. "Charlotte, Becca's right. You've been spying on everyone else, so I'm not sure you have a right to be mad. And I think Becca's been feeling a little neglected. But I can understand that you might feel surprised to find your two best friends under your porch. Why don't the three of you just sit down and talk for a few minutes? I'm sure you can work this out without fighting."

Grudgingly, the girls sat down on the porch steps together. After a few silent minutes had passed, they began to talk. "How long have you been spying on me?" asked Charlotte.

"All afternoon," answered Becca. "We followed you to my house and to the Rodowskys' and everything."

"Really?" asked Charlotte. Claudia winced, thinking Charlotte might be about to get angry again. But instead, after considering the information for a moment, Charlotte smiled. "You guys must be pretty good spies," she said. "I never even saw you."

"But we saw my brothers," said Vanessa, "and Matt and Haley. Isn't it funny how everybody's spying?"

Claudia decided that the girls were well on their way to making up. "I'll go fix a snack," she said. She headed into the kitchen, smiling to herself about the way things had worked out.

A few minutes later, she wasn't smiling anymore. Why? Guess!

Claudia caught the girls watching her through the kitchen window — and they caught *her* sneaking a spoonful of peanut butter as she made their snack.

Spy fever had gone too far.

CHAPTER 10

Sunday

Back to the mystery notebook! Mary
Anne and I had a verrrry interesting
meeting with Mr. Golem this
afternoon....

While Claudia was dealing with her young spies, Mary Anne and I were deep into detective work. I'd had a call from Reinhart Golem first thing on Sunday morning. He'd asked me to come meet him to "discuss the case" further. Actually, he invited me and a friend to brunch at his favorite restaurant, Chez Maurice. "I'm a regular there," he explained. "Whenever I'm in town I eat most of my meals at Chez Maurice."

Whoa. Now I knew for sure that the guy was rich. I mean, I'd have to save up my baby-sitting earnings for months just to be able to buy myself one dinner at that place. And he ate there all the time? No wonder he could afford to offer us a juicy reward. Anyway, I knew there was no way my mom and Watson would agree to that plan (and they'd be sure to notice if I tried to leave the house all dressed up), so Mary Anne and I ended up going out to Golem's house instead.

"Welcome, welcome," he said as he ushered us into his huge dining room. "I had my caterer bring over a little snack for us. Please help yourselves."

Mary Anne and I exchanged a glance. This was like going to Chez Maurice without having to dress up. The dining room was just as fancy. The dark, highly polished table was set with beautiful china and silver, and green velvet curtains hung at the leaded-glass windows. The food looked every bit as good. Laid out on a side table were giant platters heaped with pastries; huge silver chafing dishes filled with eggs, bacon, and sausage; and bowls of the most beautiful fruit. Mary Anne and I filled our plates and sat down.

"This is delicious," I said after a few bites. I was feeling a little nervous.

"It is," Mary Anne agreed. "Thank you very much."

Golem chuckled. "It's the least I could do for my star detectives. I'm convinced you'll solve this case before the police do. I have a good feeling about you young ladies."

I blushed. "Well, we've been working on it," I said, "and a few clues have surfaced. For example, did you know that one of your own neighbors in New York was robbed by the Cat Burglar?"

Golem looked surprised. "Now, aren't you the clever ones to dig up that bit of information. Yes, I do seem to remember something about that, though I believe I was away in France at the time." He paused. "However, I'd advise that you not spend too much time pursuing the Cat Burglar angle. From what Sergeant Winters tells me, it's possible that the cat stencil found on my mailbox was a forgery."

I glanced at Mary Anne. Hmm. Our idea about a copycat burglar might just be on target.

"What about the other evidence we found?" I asked. "Like the bullet casing and the marker?"

"The bullet casing, as you may already know, came from the same model gun that our local police force carries." He frowned, but didn't say anything more about that. "And the marker? Sergeant Winters tells me that fingerprint tests on it are almost finished, but there's nothing conclusive to report yet."

"Meanwhile, there are no leads on the diamonds," I said. "You must be upset about that."

He waved a hand. "Certainly, they were special gems. But as far as the value goes, they were heavily insured. I won't suffer any financial loss."

"That's good," said Mary Anne, sounding relieved.

He smiled at her. "So nice to know that someone cares," he said. "The police don't seem to understand how traumatic this has been for me. Can you imagine? They actually called me in for questioning."

"Oh, the've asked everyone to come in," said Mary Anne comfortingly. "Kristy had to go, and so did this other friend of ours."

We ate and talked and ate some more, and before long we were chatting like old friends.

In fact, I felt comfortable enough to ask Golem more about Ben Birch, even though I knew the subject was a sore one with him. He didn't reveal much about his old business associate, but I did find out where Birch was originally from (Cleveland), and where he was living now (possibly in Miami).

By the time Mary Anne and I left, full of eggs and bacon and information, we felt ready to get serious about catching the Cat Burglar — or the Copycat. Golem believed in us, and his confidence was contagious.

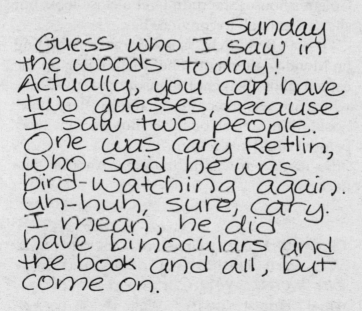

Guess who I saw in the woods today! Sunday Actually, you can have two guesses, because I saw two people. One was Cary Retlin, who said he was bird-watching again. Uh-huh, sure, Cary. I mean, he did have binoculars and the book and all, but come on.

Abby, like all of us, has a hard time taking Cary's word for anything. There's just something about him that makes you think he's up to no good. For example, the fact that he's often up to no good. So I couldn't blame her for being suspicious about what Cary was doing in the woods near Reinhart Golem's house. Abby was cruising around on her bike, just "checking out the scene," later on the same day Mary Anne and I had visited Golem. But it wasn't the Cary Retlin sighting that really raised her suspicions.

Abby saw someone else that day too. A shadowy figure in the woods near Reinhart Golem's house. She didn't get a close look, but she saw enough to convince her.

"It was Ben Birch," she said at our meeting on Monday afternoon. She was holding up the copied photo Sergeant Johnson had given me, which we were keeping in the mystery notebook. "I'm almost positive. But he ran away before I could talk to him."

So Ben Birch was in the area. Another suspect.

Monday
Okay, brace yourselves. Here's some very, very interesting news. Did you ever wonder why Cary knows so much about guns? Well, it all makes sense when you know what his father used to do....

Stacey had decided that we really ought to know more about Cary Retlin, especially after Abby spotted him in the woods. So what did she do? She invited herself over to his house pretending she wanted to learn more about birds and bird-watching.

Cary seemed surprised at her interest, but he was happy to show her his bird-watching journals and explain how he kept track of every bird he'd ever spotted. Stacey felt bad for doubting that he had really been bird-watching in the woods.

Once inside the Retlin house, Stacey scoped out every scrap of information she could. She even asked Mrs. Retlin innocent questions about where the family had lived before they moved to Stoneybrook. And she checked out every family picture on the wall. That's how she found out that Mr. Retlin, who now works as a locksmith, was once a police officer.

"There was a picture of him in uniform," she told us later. "And it turns out he was a policeman until Cary was almost eight. Then he decided he'd had enough of dangerous work and quit the force."

"So *that's* why Cary knew about the bullet casings," I mused. "I wonder if he knows about alarm systems and stuff too."

"Are you saying —?" Mal began.

"That Cary is the Cat Burglar?" I asked. "No. But I don't think we can rule him out as a suspect in the theft of the diamonds."

Stacey agreed. "Cary is hiding something," she said. "The more I learn about him, the more I have this feeling that he knows more than he's letting on."

Tuesday

Kristy, I noticed some new information about Ben Birch in your mystery notebook. notes from your fancy brunch with Golem. So I decided to follow up and see if I could find out more.

Unfortunately, Jessi didn't have much luck. She spent over an hour on her family's computer, using the Internet to try to track down Ben Birch, based on what Golem had told me about where he had come from and where he lived now. But she couldn't turn up a speck of information. Which only underlined my impression that Ben Birch was a shady character.

Claudia spent an hour or so at the library on Tuesday night, checking through old issues of the *Stoneybrook News*. Why? Because she remembered something Officer Hopkins had said on the day we found the bullet casing at Reinhart Golem's house. Officer Hopkins had mentioned Sergeant Johnson's knowing the layout of Reinhart Golem's place because he'd once worked on another case there. Claudia wondered if finding out more about that case would help us understand this one. Instead, the information she found made her even more confused.

"It turns out that a couple of years ago Sergeant Johnson started to investigate Golem for being involved in smuggling or something like that," Claudia told me when she called that night. "But the investigation was dropped because it turned out there was 'no cause' for it."

"Weird," I said. "What kind of crime would Reinhart Golem have been involved in?"

"That's the point," said Claudia. "I guess

he wasn't. But somehow Sergeant Johnson thought he was. Maybe he has something against Golem. Anyway, the incident must have made Sergeant Johnson look pretty bad. He might still be angry about it."

"Angry enough to stage a big burglary?" I asked, guessing at Claudia's thoughts. "That doesn't sound like the Sergeant Johnson we know."

"Maybe we don't know Sergeant Johnson as well as we thought we did," said Claudia.

At the time, I thought she was being overly suspicious. But after what I saw — or rather what I *didn't* see — the next day, I had to agree with her.

Late Wednesday afternoon, the phone rang. It was Reinhart Golem, calling with another tidbit of information for our investigation. He couldn't tell me why, he said, but he'd heard from a "reliable source" that the police were now almost sure that the stenciled cat was a forgery. He also told me that the phone call to the security guard had been traced to a cellular phone, but that *whose* phone it was had not been established. While I was on the phone with Golem, I heard the call-waiting beep. I switched to the other line. It was Sergeant Johnson, asking if I could come down to the station to answer a few more questions. I told him I could, then switched back to finish up with Golem. I told him where I was going and promised to keep my ears and eyes wide open for clues. He reminded me about the reward he was offering — as if I needed a reminder!

Sergeant Johnson met me in the lobby of the police station. He looked as if he hadn't been sleeping well. "Hi, Kristy. Thanks for coming," he said as he led me to his office. When we arrived at his door, he stood there for a second, scratching his head.

"What is it?" I asked.

"I could have sworn I left this shut," he said, pointing to the open door. Then he shrugged and ushered me inside, closing the door behind us. I sat down and he perched on the edge of his desk. Folding his arms, he looked at me intently and started firing questions at me, even though I didn't have a parent present. What had I told Sergeant Winters the day of the burglary? Where exactly was it that I had found that bullet casing? And the marker — where had we found that?

He seemed to be preoccupied with those points, and I didn't understand why. Then, suddenly, it became clear. I was looking at his desk as we talked, and I spotted something that gave me chills. Three somethings, to be exact. Markers, just like the one Mary Anne had found at Reinhart Golem's. A green one. A yellow one. A black one.

But no red one.

And the set belonged to Sergeant Johnson. That's when I knew Claudia was right. We didn't know Sergeant Johnson as well as we thought we did.

I cut the interview short then, telling Sergeant Johnson that I had to hurry to our BSC meeting. I was so confused that I didn't want to spend another second in that office. He tried to ask me a few more questions about Sergeant Winters and Officer Hopkins and what they'd asked me about him, but I told him I didn't have time to talk. Finally, he agreed to let me leave.

As we walked down the hall, guess who we bumped into? Sergeant Winters and Reinhart Golem.

Sergeant Johnson looked irritated. "Why is this man here without my knowledge?" he asked Sergeant Winters. "This is my investigation. If you're going to talk about it, you need to clear it with me first."

Sergeant Winters looked irritated too. "Excuse me, Sergeant. All I was doing was briefing Mr. Golem on the status of the investigation. He is, after all, the victim of a break-in and apparent burglary."

They shot angry glances at each other.

I looked at Golem. "Hi there, Kristy," he said. "We meet again." He gave me a little smile as if to assure me that everything was okay.

But everything wasn't okay. Something very strange was happening, and I didn't understand it — or like it — at all.

CHAPTER 11

"Are you *sure?*" asked Mary Anne. She looked upset. "They were really the exact same kind of markers?"

I nodded. "None of us wants to believe it, Mary Anne. You know I like Sergeant Johnson as much as anyone. But there's a lot of evidence pointing to the fact that he —"

"Don't even say it," she said, covering her ears.

I'd left the police station only half an hour earlier, and now I was in Claudia's room, in the middle of a BSC meeting. I'd been filling my friends in on what had happened during my meeting with Sergeant Johnson.

Stacey put an arm around Mary Anne. "We can't ignore evidence just because we like somebody," she said gently. "Good detectives have to be totally impartial. And if we want to solve this case and win that reward money, we're going to have to be *really* good detectives."

Claudia passed Mary Anne a miniature Butterfinger bar. "Eat this," she suggested. "It'll make you feel better."

Absently, Mary Anne peeled back the wrapper and took a bite. "I wish I'd never found that marker," she said softly.

"It's not just the marker," I reminded her. "There's the bullet casing too. I know the testing is inconclusive so far, but still. And then Claudia found out that Sergeant Johnson had investigated Golem. Plus, everyone else seems to suspect him."

"Still," Abby said, "none of this so-called evidence proves anything for sure. And we still have a bunch of other suspects, right? I mean, what about Cary?"

"I'm the first to be suspicious of Cary," I said. "But I just can't quite picture him as the Cat Burglar. I mean, why would he be robbing fancy apartments in Manhattan?"

"Maybe so he can afford really good binoculars for bird-watching," said Stacey with a giggle.

"Okay, so maybe Cary's innocent. But what about Ben Birch?" asked Abby. "I'd like to know if he has anything to do with this."

"He is a real mystery," said Jessi. "I couldn't

find any information on him at all, no matter how long I surfed the Net."

"We do need to find out more about him," I mused. "If anyone else spots him, make sure to follow him. Maybe we can figure out where he lives and what he's up to in Stoneybrook." I dug out the photocopied picture and passed it around. Personally, I knew I'd be thrilled if Ben Birch turned out to be the Cat Burglar. I'd love to throw my suspicions about Sergeant Johnson right out the window. But I couldn't do that yet. Not if we were going to solve this case the proper way, by checking out every suspect thoroughly, even if they happened to be our friends.

The phone rang then, and we took some time out from our detective work to set up a job. Abby would be sitting for Charlotte the next day. She'd read everything in the club notebook about Charlotte's spying activities and said she was looking forward to seeing Stoneybrook's version of Harriet the Spy in action.

After that, we returned to talking about the case. "There's one more person who's still on our list," Claudia said. "That security guard. What was his name again?"

"Jack Fenton," Mal replied. "And I think he's in the clear. I haven't had a chance to write up my notes in the mystery notebook yet, but I did follow up on his alibi this afternoon."

"Really?" I asked. I was very impressed with the way the BSC members were pulling together on this case. "Cool. What did you find out?"

"Well," said Mal, "I wanted to know whether he'd really gone to the hospital that day, like he said he had. So I rode my bike to the hospital, thinking I'd snoop around and find out if his wife had been admitted. As it turned out, I didn't even have to go inside."

"Why not?" I asked.

"I saw a guard outside," Mal answered. "And the logo on his cap said Maximum Security. I remembered the name from Abby's notes, so I knew he worked for the same company as Jack Fenton. I walked right up to him and started talking. Before long, I had my answer. This guy had been on duty at the hospital that day, and he'd seen Jack come in. His wife *wasn't* there — it had been some kind of mixup — but anyway, Jack's story checked out. That was all I needed to know."

"Excellent work, Mal," I said. "Give that girl a chocolate bar!"

Claudia tossed the bag to her.

"And cross Jack Fenton off the suspect list," I added. "It sounds as if he's been cleared."

Mary Anne, the mystery notebook in her lap, made a note. She looked glum. To her the news about Jack Fenton meant that we had one less suspect, one less chance for Sergeant Johnson to be innocent. In fact, it looked even worse for our friend. Had he been the one to make a bogus phone call to Jack Fenton, to keep him away from Golem's house?

Just then, there was a knock at the door. "Come in," Claudia called. Hurriedly, she stuffed the bag of candy under her pillow.

Janine opened the door and leaned in. "Claudia, there's someone here to see you. It's a police officer, and he wants to talk to you, Kristy, and Mary Anne." She raised her eyebrows. "If I didn't know you as well as I do, I'd wonder if you were in some kind of trouble." She looked very curious.

We didn't take the time to explain. The three of us jumped up and ran downstairs.

It was Sergeant Johnson. He stood in the Kishis' front hall, mashing his hat between his hands. He looked awful, even worse than when I'd seen him at the station just an hour earlier. Then he'd looked as if he hadn't been sleeping well. Now he looked as if he hadn't slept at all — for weeks. He had dark circles under his eyes, his hair was mussed, and his uniform was wrinkled.

"Sergeant Johnson!" Mary Anne cried. "Are you all right?"

He didn't answer her directly. "Hello, girls,"

he said. His voice sounded hollow. "I just came by to ask you a few more questions."

"Come into the living room," said Claudia.

When we were seated, Sergeant Johnson began to talk. He asked the same questions he'd asked me earlier, about the evidence we'd found and about what the other officers had said about him. We answered his questions as well as we could, but he didn't seem satisfied. Instead of standing up, thanking us, and leaving, he just sat there, twisting his hat in his hands.

Then his radio went off. Through the crackle of static, we heard a voice ask for his "twenty."

"That means his location," hissed Claudia as Sergeant Johnson answered the call. "I remember from one of those police shows."

Sergeant Johnson spoke into his radio, giving Claudia's address. Then he sat back on the couch. He looked utterly miserable. "I just don't understand," he said in a distant voice. "I haven't done anything wrong. You believe me, don't you?"

"I do," said Mary Anne, jumping up to sit beside him on the couch.

Claudia and I remained silent, but Sergeant Johnson didn't seem to notice. He began to talk. I had the feeling he had reached the end of his rope, and that he wasn't so much talking to us as thinking out loud. It was pretty upsetting to see him act so strange. But the three of us sat there and listened as he rambled on.

"What I don't understand is how that evidence turned up when it did," he said. "I mean, we searched the house and grounds from top to bottom after that incident and found nothing. Then — presto! — some kids come along and turn up major stuff. Bullet casings. Markers. Where did that evidence come from? That's what I don't understand. And why are they trying to make me look bad? They're asking people about me, making me look like some kind of a criminal. I bet it's Winters. He knows I'm up for the chief's job when the chief retires. He wants that job himself. And Hopkins? She's hoping Winters will promote her if he becomes the big cheese. They're all against me. All of them. They took that marker right off my desk when I was out. That's why my fingerprints are all over it. Can't you just see Winters doing that? I'm telling you, it's a frame-up."

The three of us exchanged looks. I felt terrible for Sergeant Johnson, but I didn't know what to say to him. Were the things he was saying true? Or was he just covering up?

I'll tell you one thing: I didn't like the way he talked about our finding the evidence, as if we were just some kids off the street. Didn't he

106

trust our detective skills? He could have shown a little more respect for us after all the cases we'd helped him solve.

I felt confused. His behavior was *really* weird. It was almost as if he wanted to plant ideas in our heads about his being framed. Did he expect us to parrot it all back to someone? He seemed to want something from us, but I didn't know what it was. I could see that Claudia and Mary Anne felt just as confused and scared as I did.

I opened my mouth to speak — not that I knew what I was going to say — but then I heard a knock at the front door. Claudia jumped up to answer it, and returned moments later, followed by the chief of police. His name is John Pierce, and he's a big, barrel-chested man with thick black hair and a very serious manner.

He was even more serious than usual that day as he walked across the room to Sergeant Johnson. "Sergeant James Johnson," he began, "you have the right to remain silent —"

Mary Anne gasped. Claudia and I did too.

Sergeant Johnson was being arrested.

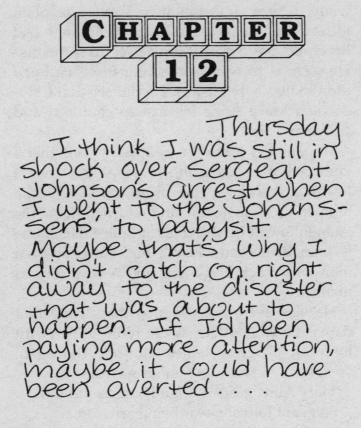

CHAPTER 12

Thursday

I think I was still in shock over Sergeant Johnson's arrest when I went to the Johanssens' to babysit. Maybe that's why I didn't catch on right away to the disaster that was about to happen. If I'd been paying more attention, maybe it could have been averted. . . .

Sergeant Johnson's arrest was the lead story in the morning's papers. Abby's mom pointed it out to her. "Isn't this that police officer you know?" she asked, showing her the picture of Sergeant Johnson on the front page.

"Wow!" Anna said. "Is he in trouble? I thought he was a good guy."

"He is," Abby replied. "At least, I always thought he was," she added softly. She stuck a bagel into the toaster, then read quickly through the first part of the article. Apparently, there was quite a bit of evidence indicating that Sergeant Johnson had been involved, somehow, in the burglary at Reinhart Golem's.

Such as the velvet bag containing two diamonds that was found in Sergeant Johnson's desk.

Abby groaned when she read that. The story also mentioned the red marker Mary Anne had found and said that some of the fingerprints on it had been identified as Sergeant Johnson's. There was a quote from Golem about the "brilliant young detective" who had discovered that piece of evidence.

The story did not go so far as to say that Sergeant Johnson was guilty, but it sure did make him look bad. It even mentioned a suspicious cell phone call, though it said that the records proving its origin were yet to be found.

Abby couldn't get over it. "It just doesn't add up," she told Anna. "There's something wrong about all this."

She thought about it on the way over to the Johanssens'. When she arrived, she tried to put it out of her mind and concentrate on sitting, but it wasn't easy. Even Charlotte had heard about the arrest, and she was confused, wondering how a police officer could do anything wrong. "I thought the police were supposed to take care of us," she said. "If they do wrong things too, maybe we're not so safe."

"We don't know for sure that Sergeant Johnson did anything wrong," said Abby. "But anyway, the police *are* here to protect us, and that's what they'll do. You don't have to worry about that." Abby hoped she sounded reassuring.

"Okay," said Charlotte. "Can Vanessa and Becca come over?"

Relieved that it had been so simple to ease Charlotte's worries, Abby agreed. Charlotte ran off to call her friends.

The girls hurried over and headed up to Charlotte's room. Abby heard a lot of giggling through the closed door and wondered what they were up to. But Charlotte had made it clear that Abby wasn't invited to join her and her friends, so Abby stayed downstairs, listening to the radio in the living room in hopes of hearing more news about Sergeant Johnson's arrest.

Soon, Abby heard the girls pounding down the stairs. "Can we go out?" asked Charlotte. "We won't go far."

Abby looked up to see Charlotte and her friends wearing identical red hooded sweatshirts. Each one was carrying a backpack and had hung a flashlight from her belt. It wasn't hard to guess what they were planning to do. But Abby knew that the girls were allowed to play on their own as long as they didn't leave the neighborhood, so she said, "Sure. Just be careful."

"We will!" called Charlotte as she led her friends out the door.

Abby watched them leave, then made a quick decision. She was supposed to be babysitting, wasn't she? And even though her charge wasn't exactly a baby, Abby was being paid to keep an eye on her. So, would there really be anything wrong with — following her around?

She didn't have a red sweatshirt, and there was no flashlight attached to her belt. But Abby was going to spy on the spies.

She followed them down the street, match ing their speed and stopping when they stopped, ducking from tree to tree in order to avoid being seen if they happened to look back.

First stop was the Mancusis'. Abby watched as the three girls huddled behind a tree to observe Pooh Bear, who was in the yard playing with a giant blue ball. At first her attention was on the girls, but then she began to notice that, using his nose and paws, Pooh Bear was moving the ball around like a soccer player. She hadn't known that a dog could play soccer. She became so engrossed in watching that she almost missed seeing Charlotte, Becca, and Vanessa take off for the next spot on Charlotte's rounds: the Rodowskys' house.

Jackie and his brothers were in their yard, playing catch with a Frisbee. Charlotte and her friends arranged themselves behind a row of bushes, while Abby crouched behind a car in the neighbor's driveway. The boys were having too much fun to notice that four people were watching their every move. Abby was amazed at the catches they could make: between the legs, over the shoulder, diving to the ground. Again, she became so interested in what she was watching that she almost forgot to keep an eye on Charlotte as well. Just in time, she noticed her band of spies moving off toward Becca's house.

There wasn't much going on at the Ramseys', though Abby caught sight of Jessi doing ballet exercises as she made herself a snack in the kitchen. She had to admit that spying was interesting and fun — and addictive. She was a little disappointed when Charlotte seemed ready to quit for the day. Still, she followed as Charlotte and her friends headed back to the Johanssens'. Abby managed to dash around to the back door as they entered in the front. She greeted them, calling out that she was in the kitchen. They trooped in, eyes sparkling and faces flushed.

"Having fun?" Abby asked innocently.

"Definitely," said Charlotte. She set her backpack on the table. "Can we have a snack?"

"Sure," said Abby. She began to rummage around in the cupboards to see what there was. "How about cereal?" she asked.

But Charlotte was checking the cookie shelf. "How about Chips Ahoy?" she asked her friends.

Becca and Vanessa were happy with that choice. Abby poured them some milk, and the girls sat down at the table to eat. Abby headed into the living room to turn on the radio and check the news.

She listened for awhile without hearing anything about Sergeant Johnson. Then, suddenly, she heard raised voices from the kitchen and decided to see what the girls were arguing about.

Charlotte's tape recorder lay in the center of the table. All three girls were talking at once. Becca and Vanessa sounded angry, and Charlotte sounded defensive.

"How could you spy on us, your best friends?" Becca was saying.

"And how could you say such mean stuff about us?" Vanessa asked.

Charlotte protested. "I didn't mean to be mean," she said weakly. "I'm sorry."

"What happened?" asked Abby.

"Ask her," said Becca. She folded her arms across her chest and stared at Charlotte.

Charlotte looked guilty. "We were — um — spying a little before," she admitted. "So we were going to listen to the tape we just made. But I must have flipped the tape over. I played the wrong side, and they heard some stuff that should have been private."

"Play it for her," said Vanessa.

Charlotte winced.

"Go on," said Becca.

Charlotte shrugged and started the tape player. Her voice echoed in the kitchen. "I don't know why Becca has to act like such a baby sometimes. She always gets her way when she wants something. Especially from her aunt Cecelia. I think Becca is spoiled."

Charlotte turned the tape player off. The kitchen was silent for a second. Then Vanessa spoke up. "Play the part about me," she said.

Charlotte didn't move. "Do I have to?" she asked Abby.

Vanessa grabbed the tape player and punched buttons until Charlotte's voice filled the room again. "Vanessa's bike is so old and creaky. She must be embarrassed because her dad's too poor to buy her a new one."

Vanessa clicked the tape player off and set it gently on the table. Then she stood up. "It's bad enough that you spied on us," she told Charlotte. "But the things you said aren't even true. Becca's not spoiled at all. In fact, Aunt Cecelia is really strict with her. And I happen to love my bike the way it is. My dad offered to buy me a new one but I didn't want it. You should be a more careful spy if you're going to keep doing it." Then she stalked out of the room. Becca followed her. Abby and Charlotte heard the front door slam.

"Just like Harriet," said Charlotte softly, staring down at the tape player. "My life is ruined."

"Not true," said Abby. "But there are three things you have to do right away." She helped Charlotte figure out what they were. One was to apologize to her friends. The other two were to destroy the tape and forget about spying for awhile.

By the end of the afternoon, thanks to Abby's

help, Charlotte and her friends were playing together again — and they weren't playing spy.

And Abby? She was thinking hard about what had happened to Charlotte. Charlotte had spied a lot, but that didn't mean she was a great spy. Likewise, the BSC members had done a lot of detective work, but that didn't make us real detectives. We'd helped to gather the evidence against Sergeant Johnson, but did the evidence really mean he was guilty? Maybe we'd been wrong to think we knew what we were doing. Maybe the idea of earning Golem's reward had made us blind to the real facts.

CHAPTER

13

Abby wasn't the only one doing some hard thinking. If you'd gone looking for me on Friday afternoon, you'd have found me in my room with the door shut, lying on my bed and just staring at the ceiling. I might have looked as if I were ready to take a nap, but that would have been far from the truth. What I was doing was thinking, thinking, and thinking some more. My brain was practically steaming from the effort.

I'd spent a lot of the day thinking about Sergeant Johnson and all the times the BSC members had worked with him. Before now, I'd never had reason to suspect him of anything. He had always been kind and honest and appreciative of everything my friends and I did. I could just picture him behind his desk or at the scene of a crime, taking in every clue in his calm, thoughtful way. He was a good listener. I thought of the way his eyes would focus on me as we went over a list of suspects or discussed a new clue.

Then I pictured the Sergeant Johnson I'd seen two days before. I remembered how bloodshot his eyes had been, how haggard his face had looked. I thought of how he'd rambled on, talking like a crazy person.

His questions rang in my ears. Why didn't the police find that bullet casing and the marker when they searched the house? Now that I thought about it, I remembered thinking it was a little odd myself — the way they were just lying out there in plain sight. Had someone placed them there *after* the search? And if so, who? Was someone trying to frame Sergeant Johnson? If so, why would he (or she) want to?

I remembered something else that afternoon, something that bothered me. It was about the timing of events on the day of the burglary. I knew it had only been a matter of minutes between the time the alarm went off and the time Sergeant Johnson had approached Karen, David Michael, and me. A few minutes in which to do all of the following:

1) Draw the red cat on the mailbox.
2) Crack the safe.
3) Grab the diamonds.
4) Leave the house.
5) Run to the spot where I was standing

without showing any sign of stress or exertion.

Even if, say, he'd drawn the cat earlier (I could have missed seeing it when I first passed the mailbox), he couldn't do all the other things in such a short period of time. Especially considering that he hadn't looked at all flushed or hurried when I first saw him. He just looked like himself, the Sergeant Johnson I knew and trusted. And his main concern was for our safety.

When I thought of that, I turned over on my bed and buried my face in my pillow. I remembered Sergeant Johnson ordering us to sit in his car and stay there until he was sure it was safe. Then I remembered that when he'd driven us home he'd turned on the lights to please David Michael.

Sergeant Johnson was a friend.

He was a good man and a good police officer.

And now he was under arrest.

I'd helped to find the evidence that led to his arrest, but now I was questioning myself. Did the evidence really add up? Maybe we'd been in too much of a hurry to solve the case and win that reward money.

"Kristy!" I heard Sam calling me from outside my door.

"Leave me alone," I called back. "I'm trying to think."

"Aww," he said. "Don't do that. You might strain your brain. Anyway, there's someone here to see you."

Oh, no. "Who?" I asked. "Is it the police?"

Sam laughed. "I don't think so," he said. "Not unless they're accepting eighth-grade wise guys on the force these days."

Huh? I rolled off my bed and headed out of my room and down the stairs.

Cary Retlin was waiting for me in the downstairs hall.

"Having a little beauty rest?" he asked me, lifting that eyebrow.

"I don't need it," I shot back, tossing my head. "Actually, I was thinking. Something you probably never do."

"That's where you're wrong. I think all the time. In fact, I'm even thinking now. I'm thinking I made a mistake to come over here." He turned to leave.

"Wait," I said. "I'm sorry." I'd never seen Cary act so sensitive. Something was bothering him. "What's up?" I sat down on the stairs and motioned for him to take a seat too.

He didn't speak for a moment. Then he began. "I read about Sergeant Johnson's arrest," he said. "It doesn't seem right. I mean, it's been fun to work on this mystery. You know my philosophy: Complications make life more interesting. But complications are one thing, and unfairness is another. I can't stop thinking about it."

"Me too!" I exclaimed. How odd, to be agreeing with Cary Retlin. "I keep going over everything in my mind. The puzzle doesn't quite fit together, but I can't put my finger on why."

"Well, maybe this will help," Cary said. "Do you remember my telling you that I thought I saw a light on in an upstairs bedroom at Reinhart Golem's house on the day of the burglary?"

I shook my head. "To be honest, I don't," I said. I was a little embarrassed. That sounded like something I should have paid attention to.

"I hardly remembered myself," Cary said. "Until the other day. Then I started thinking about it, and I haven't been able to stop."

"Tell me more," I said. I wished I had a pen and the mystery notebook handy, but I didn't, so I just listened carefully.

"Well, first of all, I saw the security guard leave the area," said Cary. "You know, through my binoculars. I really was watching birds out there."

I nodded. "Then what?"

"Then I saw this light go on upstairs in the mansion." Cary stopped again.

"And?" I prompted.

"And then I saw it go off again."

My heart started to beat a little quicker. "So that means there was someone in the house," I said. "But how do we know it wasn't Sergeant Johnson?"

Cary paused. "Because I saw him drive up a few minutes later," he said. "After the alarm went off. Before that, I can tell you for sure that nobody entered or left the house. Whoever stole those diamonds had been in there for awhile."

"This is very big news," I said. We were both silent for a moment. Then, before we could start talking again, Charlie came flying through the front door.

"Ready to go?" he asked. "Sorry I'm late. But we'll make it on time if we leave now."

I checked my watch. It was five-twenty, almost time for our BSC meeting. I turned to Cary. "Let's go," I said.

"Uh — where?" he asked.

"BSC meeting," I told him. "Everybody will be there, and we can figure this out."

"I don't know," said Cary. "Isn't it all girls and diapers and stuff?"

"Since when are you afraid of girls?" I asked. I grabbed his arm and practically pulled him out to the car. Ten minutes later, I was calling the meeting to order, and introducing our special guest.

At first Cary looked totally uncomfortable,

sitting in a dining room chair Claudia had brought from downstairs. My BSC friends were surprised to see him, and they were a little uncomfortable too — for about ten seconds. Then Abby teased him by imitating that eyebrow thing he does, and Claudia passed him a Milky Way bar and some Cheez-its, and soon we all seemed to relax. Still, having Cary in the room was weird. It just shows how far we'll go to solve a mystery! Cary leafed through the mystery notebook and read our copies of articles about the Cat Burglar while I went quickly over our BSC business. Then we started to talk about the case.

I asked him to tell everyone what he'd seen. Then we began to talk about what it meant.

Stacey understood right away. "So this could mean Sergeant Johnson was framed, right?" she asked. "I mean, he wasn't there, but somebody's trying to make it look as if he was."

"That's what I think," I said.

"But we don't know *who*," Jessi pointed out. "I mean, if Sergeant Johnson didn't steal the diamonds, who did? And is the thief framing Sergeant Johnson, or is it someone else?"

"Whoever's framing him had to have access to his desk," mused Mary Anne. "Because he stole that marker, and put the diamonds there too."

"He had to have access to Sergeant Johnson's

gun too," Cary pointed out. "Or one just like it."

"Okay, so someone who can come and go at the police station, someone who has something against Sergeant Johnson," I said. I felt a little shiver go down my spine. "Someone like Sergeant Winters." Suddenly, Sergeant Johnson's words came back to me. He'd been trying to tell us, but we hadn't believed him.

The room was silent for a second.

Then Mal spoke up. "Sergeant Winters?" she repeated. "But he's a police officer."

"An extremely ambitious police officer," Cary said slowly, looking at me intently. "A police officer who does not seem too fond of his main competition for the chief's job."

So he'd heard about that too. I nodded. "There's definitely a lot of tension between Sergeant Johnson and Sergeant Winters," I said. "Whatever the reason."

"Kristy's right," Cary told the others. "You should have seen them when they met in the hall the other day. They were snapping at each other like angry dogs."

"Sergeant Winters would have had access to Sergeant Johnson's office," said Mary Anne.

I remembered the last time I'd been at the station, when Sergeant Johnson swore he'd left the door shut. "No question about it," I said.

"So he could have taken the marker and

planted the diamonds," said Abby. "But what about the evidence you found at Golem's house? Did he plant that?"

"I bet he did," said Claudia excitedly. She turned to me. "Don't you remember? We saw Sergeant Winters leaving there the day we found the bullet casing and the marker."

"I remember," said Mary Anne. "He could easily have planted them then."

"Wow," breathed Mal. "This is wild. But what about his motive? Did he do it just because he wants the chief's job?"

"Maybe," said Abby slowly. "Or maybe not. Remember, we don't know anything about him. He came from somewhere else. We don't even know where. Maybe he's the Cat Burglar!"

We all stopped talking to think about that idea. At first it sounded totally nuts, but the more I considered it, the more sense it made. I didn't know if it was true. How could I? But I did know that we had to tell someone what we'd figured out.

"Who can we talk to about this?" I asked my friends. "I mean, we can't talk to Sergeant Winters, obviously. And Sergeant Johnson isn't available."

Mary Anne spoke up. "What about Reinhart Golem?" she asked shyly.

"That's it," I cried. "Perfect. He'll take us seriously, and after all, he has a real interest in this case. He wouldn't want to see the wrong person go to jail." I reached for the phone. "What's his number? It's on his card, in the mystery notebook."

Mary Anne found it and read it to me. I dialed, but there was no answer.

"He's not home. Let's just go out there. I bet he'll be back by the time we arrive."

Mary Anne checked her watch. "But it's almost dinnertime. Maybe he's at Chez Maurice."

Within minutes, we'd made a plan and were on our way. Cary, Abby, Mary Anne, and I were headed out to Golem's house. The others would go to Chez Maurice. We'd find Reinhart Golem, wherever he was. And soon we'd be on our way to clearing Sergeant Johnson's name.

CHAPTER 14

"I think he's still out," said Abby. "I don't see a car, and the house looks all shut up."

"Bummer," Cary said.

"Let's knock anyway," Mary Anne suggested.

I stepped up to the big front door and lifted the heavy brass knocker. I let it fall three times. *Bang. Bang. Bang.* The sound seemed to echo inside the house.

We waited for a few seconds. Nothing happened.

"Now what do we do?" asked Abby. "Should we —"

She was interrupted in midthought when the door suddenly swung open.

"Why, what a lovely surprise!" Golem stood there looking down at us. He was dressed in what I think is called a "smoking jacket," a cross between a blazer and a fancy bathrobe. It was made of dark blue velvet and had satin lapels. On his feet were matching blue velvet slippers. He had a cigar in one hand and a glass of something — brandy? — in the other. He was smiling broadly.

"I was just relaxing in the parlor. Won't you join me?" He led us through the front hall and into a cozy room at the back corner of the house.

The room was dimly lit. A cushy-looking couch and several overstuffed armchairs, all covered in green velvet, were arranged around the room. Heavy green velvet curtains shut out the late afternoon light. A silver tray holding crystal glasses and a silver ice bucket sat on a highly polished table.

"Can I offer you a beverage?" asked Golem. For one wild second I thought he was going to pour us each a glass of brandy. "Some spring water, perhaps? Or fruit juice?"

"We're really just here to talk," I said. "Thanks, though."

He waved a hand. "Shall we sit, then?" he asked. "I know you must have something of great interest to share. I just wanted to make sure everyone was comfortable."

We each took a seat. Cary and I ended up on the couch, while Mary Anne and Abby sat in chairs opposite us. Golem sat in the last chair, the one farthest from the fireplace and nearest to the door. "Lovely," he murmured. "I'm so glad you're here. I was just going to call and invite you all over. I understand that the culprit is behind bars, which means we have something to celebrate. And we must talk about the reward."

"Well, not quite yet," said Abby eagerly. "You may not believe this, but we think Sergeant Johnson has been framed. And we think we know who did it."

Golem raised his eyebrows. "So very interesting," he said. "Do go on."

Abby started to explain how we'd figured out that Sergeant Johnson was probably innocent. She told him about the things Sergeant Johnson had said to us just before his arrest, and how they had made us begin to wonder why the police hadn't found the evidence during their search. She explained why we had a hard time believing that Sergeant Johnson could be guilty and told Golem that something just hadn't felt right to us.

Abby was on a roll. Mary Anne was quiet, but that was nothing new. She was probably feeling shy. And even I couldn't fit a word in edgewise. In fact, I was a little irritated that Abby had taken over. After all, I knew Reinhart Golem better than she did. But the important thing then was to put all the facts on the table, and I had to admit she was doing a fine job of that. So far, I had nothing to add.

Then Abby started to explain how Cary had remembered the light he'd seen in the house. I turned to look at him, wondering why he wasn't chiming in with his own story. He'd been nearly silent since we'd entered the room.

His face was pale. And he wasn't looking at Abby. He didn't seem to be hearing a word she said. What was the matter with Cary? I almost interrupted Abby to ask him, but instinct made me wait. Instead, I followed his glance. He was staring at something across the room, staring hard.

I looked to see what had captured his interest. That's when I saw it.

Sitting on a side table behind Mary Anne and Abby was — a lamp. But it wasn't just any lamp.

It was a blue Tiffany lamp.

Just like the one we'd read that the Cat Burglar had stolen.

I checked to see if anyone had seen me looking at it. Abby was still chattering away, and she was looking at Golem. He was looking right back at her, nodding as he puffed on his cigar. Mary Anne was watching him.

I glanced at Cary. He wasn't looking at the lamp anymore. Our eyes met for a split second, and I saw that he and I were thinking the same thing.

My head was spinning. Abby was still talking to Golem, listing all our evidence and explaining the process that had led us to believe that Sergeant Winters had framed Sergeant Johnson.

But as she talked I realized something. It wasn't Sergeant Winters at all.

"So then we figured out that it had to be somebody who had access to Sergeant Johnson's desk," Abby said.

But Sergeant Winters wasn't the only one who had access, I thought. I remembered that Sergeant Johnson's office door had been open when he questioned me about finding the marker. *Golem was in the building that day too, talking to Sergeant Winters. And that was the day the diamonds were found in Sergeant Johnson's desk.*

"And we remembered hearing how badly Sergeant Winters wants to be promoted to chief," Abby was saying.

What about the marker? When could Golem have taken that? I tried to put it together in my mind. Then I remembered Golem's saying he'd been called in for questioning early on in the case. *He could have grabbed it then and planted it at his house before we came out that day. Of course, he didn't know who would find it, but he knew someone would.*

"I mean, he came from who-knows-where to join the dinky little Stoneybrook police force," Abby was saying.

But Golem was in France when the burglary took place. Wasn't he? I glanced at Cary again and thought about the light he'd seen in an upstairs bedroom that day.

"So, Kristy thinks that it's even possible that Sergeant Winters is the Cat Burglar," Abby said. "Right, Kristy?"

I didn't hear her. I was lost in my thoughts. I was staring at that blue Tiffany lamp, thinking madly.

"Kristy?"

I looked away from the lamp — and right into Reinhart Golem's eyes. They looked dark now, almost black. I gulped. He'd seen me looking at the lamp, no question about it.

But had he figured out that I had figured things out?

"Um — right," I said, answering Abby. "Listen, I think we'd better head on out now, guys."

"What?" Abby looked completely confused.

"Now?" asked Mary Anne. She was bewildered too. "Why?"

"Um," I said, stalling. I couldn't think of a good excuse.

Cary jumped in. "Don't you remember, we told the others we'd meet them?" he said, putting a special edge in his voice, as if to tell Abby and Mary Anne to go along with what he was saying.

"We did?" asked Abby.

Mary Anne caught on. "Oh, right," she said carefully, giving Abby a little look. "I remember now. We did."

Abby still looked confused. "Okay," she said. "Whatever."

Cary stood up, and I did too. Abby and Mary Anne followed our lead. We all began to walk toward the door.

"It was delightful having you all," said Golem. "Your detective work has been excellent, as always. I'll have to explore the new angle you've brought up." He didn't rise from his seat. Instead, he moved his right hand over to a small black box that sat on a table next to his chair. He touched a button on the box and we heard a small *click.*

Cary was near the door by then. He reached for the knob and turned it. Or, at least, he tried to.

"It's locked," he whispered. His face was totally white as he looked back at the rest of us.

"So unlock it," Abby said.

"I can't," said Cary. "We're trapped."

CHAPTER 15

I whirled to face Golem. "Let us out of here!" I said.

"I'm afraid that won't be possible," Golem answered calmly. By now he was standing, facing us. "You know too much."

"Too much about what?" I asked, trying to sound innocent.

He just laughed. I saw his glance slide toward the blue lamp and back to me. "I have a flight booked to Paris in, let's see," — he shot out a wrist to check his watch — "four hours. Until I leave, you'll all have to stay here with me."

"But," Abby said, "I don't understand."

"I'm sure your friend will be happy to explain," said Golem. Smirking, he gave me a mock bow.

I was furious. "It's him!" I said. "He's the Cat Burglar. He's the one who framed Sergeant

Johnson, and he used *us* to do it. He hid in his own house and stole his own diamonds. He faked a burglary and planted those clues for us — or someone else — to find. And he probably manipulated Sergeant Winters and Officer Hopkins too."

"Very good," said Golem smoothly. He seemed totally unruffled, which made me even angrier.

"You're going to be in trouble if you keep us here against our wishes," said Cary.

Golem just raised his eyebrows. "I'll be halfway across the ocean before anyone even figures out where you are."

I heard a stifled sob and looked at Mary Anne. "It's okay," I told her.

"It certainly is," said Golem. "Once I'm safely gone, you'll eventually be discovered and freed. Then everyone will be happy." He smiled and touched the tips of his fingers together. "Now, let's see. I suppose I'll need some rope." He turned to open a closet door.

Everything happened very quickly after that.

The second Golem's eyes weren't on him, Cary lunged for the box with the button. If he could reach it, he'd be able to unlock the door. But Cary had only taken a step or two before Golem whirled around and ran to block him.

I heard Mary Anne gasp as Golem knocked

Cary to the floor. Cary pulled Golem down as he dropped, and the two of them wrestled for a moment.

Somehow I managed to make myself move. Three big steps brought me to the box and I reached for the button. I pushed it and heard a satisfying *click*. "Try the door!" I yelled to Abby.

But my voice was nearly drowned out by the sound of sirens. The police! Did they know how badly we needed them?

Golem swore as he struggled to his feet. But he wasn't quick enough to stop Mary Anne and Abby, who were out the door in a flash. It closed again behind them.

He glared at me. He wasn't unruffled now. In fact, his smoking jacket was torn, his hair was standing up in spikes, and he had a scratch on his cheek. Also he was angry. Very, very angry.

"Cary, come on," I said, reaching down a hand to help him up. Cary looked awful. There was a gash across his forehead and his face was white. "Let's get out of here."

My words seemed to jolt Golem into action. "Out of here!" he said. "What an excellent idea." He glanced wildly at the door and then at the curtained windows. I could tell he was desperate to escape before the police found him.

Too late. The pounding of feet told me —

and Golem — that the police were storming the house.

"In here!" I heard Abby shout, from just outside the door. Two seconds later, Chief Pierce burst into the room.

He glanced at Cary and me but headed straight for Golem. "You're under arrest," he said.

I expected Golem to try to make a break for it, or smooth talk the chief. Instead, he just nodded. Wearily, he held out his hands, and the chief snapped a pair of handcuffs onto his wrists. "You have the right to remain silent," Chief Pierce began.

Cary and I exchanged a glance. He was standing by then, and he and I nodded at each other in agreement. Then we turned and slipped out of the room.

Guess who was standing in the hall? Every member of the BSC. Not just Mary Anne and Abby but Stacey, Claudia, Mal, and Jessi too. Mary Anne rushed to Cary's side. "Are you okay?" She touched his forehead gently. "You're bleeding."

"Am I?" he asked. "It doesn't really hurt. I'm okay." He sounded dazed.

"What are all of you doing here?" I asked.

"It's a long story," said Stacey.

Just then the chief walked by, with Reinhart Golem ahead of him.

Golem scowled at us.

"Why don't you all head out now," the chief said gently. "We'll be in touch."

"Let's go back to my house for an emergency meeting," I proposed. "Cary, you come too. We'll clean up that cut and bandage it for you."

"We can order a pizza," said Stacey. "There's plenty of money in the treasury."

Half an hour later, we were happily pigging out on a large extra-cheese pie.

And we were talking. Putting all the pieces together.

First, Cary and I explained to Mary Anne and Abby about the lamp, and how seeing it had made us understand the truth about Reinhart Golem.

"Boy, was I confused," said Abby. "I didn't know what you were talking about when you said we had to leave. Now I see. But what I still don't understand is how the police knew to come."

"We told them you might be in trouble," said Claudia.

"But how did you know that?" asked Mary Anne.

"Because we went to Chez Maurice," said Stacey. "Golem wasn't there, obviously. But while Stacey was talking to the maître d', Jessi decided to flip through the reservation book."

"And I saw Reinhart Golem's name in there for the day of the burglary!" said Jessi. "When he was supposedly in France. An alarm went off in my head."

"So we went to the police station." Stacey took over the story. "Officer Hopkins was there, and we told her what we'd found out. She'd started to suspect that Golem was manipulating Sergeant Winters, so she asked us to tell our story to the chief."

Mal jumped in. "When he heard that the four of you were at Golem's house, he took immediate action. He rounded up a team and we rode over with them, with everybody's sirens blasting."

"It was pretty cool," Claudia said.

"Wow," I said, shaking my head. "I just can't believe it."

"You can't believe that Golem was caught?" asked Stacey.

"No," I said. "I can't believe how I fell for all his flattery." I felt like such a fool. "He really tricked us."

"I guess he tricked a lot of people," said Stacey comfortingly. "On the way to his place, the chief told me they'd just discovered that Ben Birch was actually one of Golem's aliases. He disguised himself all the time. We heard that the Cat Burglar was good at that, remember?"

"So that was actually Golem in the woods that day!" said Abby. "Not Ben Birch."

"Well, both, I guess," I said. "Now I see why Golem looked familiar to me." I put down my slice of pizza and reached for the mystery notebook. I pulled out Ben Birch's picture and examined it closely. Sure enough, I could see Reinhart Golem, now that I knew.

"That's why there weren't any traces of Birch on the Internet or in the papers," said Mal.

"Back to Golem," said Cary. "What about his motives? I mean, why would he rob himself — and why frame Sergeant Johnson?"

"He robbed himself so he could cash in on his insurance money and still have the diamonds," I said. I'd figured that out right away. "And he framed Sergeant Johnson with a couple of the diamonds because he was mad about being investigated that other time."

"It's all coming together. He went to a lot of trouble to make Sergeant Johnson look bad," mused Mary Anne. "He made sure Sergeant Johnson would be the first on the scene, by making that anonymous call that brought him to the neighborhood. He must have stolen a police pistol in order to shoot off the gun and leave a casing. And he made the call that sent Jack Fenton to the hospital, and took that marker and planted the diamonds —"

"Plus, he figured out that it would be easy to

turn Sergeant Winters against Sergeant Johnson," said Abby. "Whew. This guy is really something."

"He sure is," I said quietly. I was still in shock from the events of the evening. And I was scared. I mean, Cary was okay. He was just bruised and cut up. But what if Golem had used a gun? What if the police hadn't shown up? We could have been in big, big trouble.

"You know what I think?" asked Mary Anne. She still hadn't finished her pizza, and now she put it down. "I think maybe we should just concentrate on baby-sitting for awhile. Maybe this detective stuff is a little too dangerous."

I saw Stacey and Claudia nod. Jessi and Mal seemed to agree, and so did Abby.

Just then, the phone rang. I picked it up. "Baby-sitters Club," I said. It was Sergeant Johnson. He'd been freed from custody, and he was calling to thank us.

"*Thank* us?" I said. I couldn't believe my ears. "But we're the reason you were in trouble in the first place. We thought we'd stumbled on some major evidence, but it was just a set-up."

"Don't be silly," Sergeant Johnson told me. "It wasn't your fault. You were doing your best, but you ran into a very, very smart criminal."

"Well, I'm still sorry you had to go through all of that," I said.

"I am too," he replied. "But it's over now. And everything worked out okay, this time."

"Thanks for being so nice," I said. It didn't seem like enough, but I couldn't think of anything else to say.

"That's okay. Just do me one favor, Kristy."

"Sure."

"Stay out of trouble for awhile, all right?" I could tell that Sergeant Johnson was smiling.

"We will," I promised. I said good-bye, hung up, and told my friends what he'd said.

That's when we made a unanimous decision. The case of the Cat Burglar would be the BSC's last mystery.

At least for now.

Ann M. Martin

About the Author

ANN MATTHEWS MARTIN was born on August 12, 1955. She grew up in Princeton, NJ, with her parents and her younger sister, Jane.

Although Ann used to be a teacher and then an editor of children's books, she's now a full-time writer. She gets ideas for her books from many different places. Some are based on personal experiences. Others are based on childhood memories and feelings. Many are written about contemporary problems or events.

All of Ann's characters, even the members of the Baby-sitters Club, are made up. (So is Stoneybrook.) But many of her characters are based on real people. Sometimes Ann names her characters after people she knows, other times she chooses names she likes.

In addition to the Baby-sitters Club books, Ann Martin has written many other books for children. Her favorite is *Ten Kids, No Pets* because she loves big families and she loves animals. Her favorite Baby-sitters Club book is *Kristy's Big Day*. (By the way, Kristy is her favorite baby-sitter!)

Ann M. Martin now lives in New York with her cats, Gussie, Woody, and Willy. Her hobbies are reading, sewing, and needlework — especially making clothes for children.

Read all the books
about **Kristy**
in the Baby-sitters Club series
by Ann M. Martin

THE BABY-SITTERS CLUB®

by Ann M. Martin

Collect and read these exciting BSC Super Specials, Mysteries, and Super Mysteries along with your favorite Baby-sitters Club books!

BSC Super Specials

BSC Mysteries

More titles ➡

The Baby-sitters Club books continued...

Available wherever you buy books...or use this order form.

Scholastic Inc., P.O. Box 7502, 2931 East McCarty Street, Jefferson City, MO 65102-7502

Please send me the books I have checked above. I am enclosing $ _____
(please add $2.00 to cover shipping and handling). Send check or money order
— no cash or C.O.D.s please.

Name_____ Birthdate_____

Address _____

City_____ State/Zip_____

Please allow four to six weeks for delivery. Offer good in the U.S. only. Sorry, mail orders are not
available to residents of Canada. Prices subject to change.   BSCM1297